Free-Wrench

Joseph R. Lallo

To Angela
Enjoy!
Joseph Lallo

ISBN: 1505795079
ISBN-13: 978-1505795073

Dedication

This book is dedicated to the handful of wonderful fans who have given me fan art over the years. Katie, Lily, Mexe and any I have shamefully forgotten, this one's for you.

Acknowledgment

I'd like to, as always, acknowledge my fantastic cover artist Nick Deligaris, and the aforementioned fan artist Lily, who guided me to create Nita Graus when she asked me to create a character she could cosplay as.

Intro

Caldera was a chain of islands just about as far from any major continent as was geographically possible, and that suited its people just fine. The prevailing opinion about their neighboring countries was that they were vicious, brutish places of savagery and debauchery. A long stretch of choppy sea between them made for good peace of mind. As the name would suggest, Caldera wasn't so much an archipelago as a set of volcanoes that one by one peeked their heads up out of the sea floor to see what all of the fuss was about. This, too, suited its people just fine. It gave them an abundance of free heat. Combined with sea water, that created plenty of steam, and steam was what made the world go round.

The largest island was called Tellahn, home to both the mightiest volcano and, where it met the sea, the largest steamworks in the whole island chain. The East Seaward Hub, as the massive facility was called, was a bustling hive of activity day and night. It supplied the bulk of the power for the island and sat at the heart of a cluster of factories and facilities that did the dirty work for the whole of the nation. The steamworks was an intricate knot of pipes and valves, perpetually muggy, soot covered, and reeking of sulfur. It was as close to hell as most Calderans could bear to imagine, but to a rare and precious few it was paradise.

Two such workers toiled in a claustrophobic hallway near the third of ten boiler chambers. Intended for pipes rather than people, little care had been put into making it hospitable. What small amount of light there was came from the dim blue flames of gas lanterns dangling from the belts of each worker. The walls had the texture of a cheese grater, still jagged from the day the tunnel had been roughly carved through the lava rock. Making it even more treacherous was the walkway, which was a warped catwalk of oiled wood. The only thing to grab on to, should a worker become unsteady, was the unforgiving wall or the scalding-hot steam pipes. Needless to say, a wise steamworker quickly learned to step lightly and surely and wore thick gloves just in case.

"Keep your eye on that meter, Nita!" cried the foreman, a stout man with his face hidden behind a pair of brass goggles. "It's running a bit high."

"I see it, Marcus," she said, pulling her gloves tight and adjusting her own goggles. Even with lenses carefully designed to keep from fogging, the moisture constantly built up. "I don't like the way these pipes are shimmying either."

As rare as it was to find someone willing to go to work in the steamworks every day, Amanita Graus was rarer still, a *woman* willing to do so. She'd been working at the steamworks since her seventeenth birthday, and in the three years since then she'd proved herself to be an asset. In most situations it might have been difficult for a woman to find a place among the primarily male workforce, but, truth be told, the steamworks was so short on staff they were happy to have anyone willing to take up some of the slack. She currently worked as a free-wrench, a laborer traded between sections and facilities to lend an extra hand where it was needed. As one of the most demanding jobs they had, it required a working knowledge in every trade in the steamworks.

"I agree. Inspect the next fifty yards of pipe toward the boiler. I want to make sure the bypass valves are clear."

Nita nodded and got to work. Despite being the rare female steamworker, she was dressed and equipped as roughly as the men were. That meant at least one layer of leather or canvas over most of her body, a pair of chunky work gloves, and a rugged pair of work boots. To maintain the various-sized nuts, she wore a bandoleer of assorted wrenches and other tools, and an array of pouches hanging from her belt, along with two holstered rods. Most men wore a reinforced back-support belt with suspenders to take the edge off of the heavy lifting so frequently a part of the job, but Nita had found that a lightly modified corset did much the same job. The only other feminine touch she'd made to her equipment was a tasteful little butterfly accent on her goggles, a gift from her younger brother. The whole of the ensemble was fastened in place and held together with brass or copper rivets and buckles, as well as a prodigious number of leather belts.

The senior worker began a new order, but his voice trailed off as the usual hiss and rattle of pipes, thicker than his thigh, turned into a worrying rumble. Clumps of the sooty crust that tended to cling to every surface like frost in the early days of winter began to shake free as the vibration of the pipe became increasingly violent.

"Down! Brace for a breech!" the foreman said.

The man and woman hunkered down with their backs to the pipes and covered their heads. After a nerve-racking few seconds of escalating rumbling, a nearby pipe ruptured, sending a thunderous clap reverberating down the tunnel and throwing the workers against the catwalk. Steam came rushing out of a foot-long fault in the pipe, filling the tunnel with a thick fog and a deafening whistle. Nita fought her way to her feet. Acting on raw training, she grabbed a wrench and began to tap on the pipe. Since a good hard rap on the pipe could be heard throughout half of the mountain, the workers had developed a simple tap code to communicate. She listed off their status: two workers, tunnel 3A, major breech, no injuries. As soon as she was through, she heard the message begin to echo back, a nearby worker pounding it out again to acknowledge and spread the word. Next she found the pressure gauge.

"It is still climbing!" she called out on the off chance that she might be heard. "We've got to reach the bypass, or we could lose the whole boiler and half the mountain!"

She banged out this information as well, then charged down the tunnel. The nearer she came to the boiler, the thicker the pipe became, joining with others that branched off toward other parts of the facility and other parts of the island. Finally she came to a point where the pipe was half as tall as she was, with a massive wheel set into it and a branching shunt pipe leading straight up through the stone above and into daylight. Her leather gloves sizzled against the wheel as she fought with it, trying to redirect the steam flow and relieve the pressure. The shunt was only beginning to sputter with released steam when the wheel suddenly spun loose, snapped free from its shaft, and clattered to the floor.

Nita didn't waste a moment uttering any of the profanities that flitted through her head. Instead she tugged at the coils of rope slung across her shoulders and shrugged them off, freeing the massive apparatus that they held to her back. The heavy thing hit the ground with a thunk. As heavy as it was, she always brought it with her. Her very first foreman had drummed it into her that she would never know what tool might save some time, save some work, or save her life, so best to bring them all. The sheer size of it made this tool the only one she'd considered excluding from that rule. As large as a backpack and made from a dull purple-gray metal, it looked like the head of a pipe wrench designed for a giant. Her foreman called it a monkey-toe, and technically it was a so-called team wrench. Today she'd find out how well it worked without a team.

She spun the knurled adjustment screw, sliding the jaws open until they were wide enough to accept the square shaft of the broken wheel, then heaved it from the ground and onto the shaft. Two quick slaps to the screw spun it to tightness. Now for the hard part. Holstered like twin swords at her belt were a pair of cheater bars. She unsheathed one and slotted it into a hole on the head of the monkey-toe, then threw her weight against the freshly installed lever. It didn't budge, and the telltale ricochet of bursting nuts and bolts warned her that there wasn't much more time to waste. She grasped an overhead pipe and hauled herself up to plant her boots on the lever and force it with all of her weight and strength.

A grinding sound rattled along the pipe as the valve grudgingly slid open. Steam began to erupt from the top of the pipe in burps and hisses, knocking free the bubbling muck that had filled the pipe in the years since it had last been used. Three more steamworkers rushed into the tunnel from the boiler side and spotted her working at the valve. One grabbed the end of her bar to lend a hand while the other two inserted a bar of their own into the opposite end of the wrench. Their combined effort finally wrestled the valve fully open, and a geyser of stagnant water sprayed from the pipe above, followed by a column of steam that nearly reached the clouds.

Nita and her fellow workers breathed a collective sigh of relief and wiped away the coating of gunk that was still raining down through the opening above them.

"Well," Nita said, pulling out a clean handkerchief from a pouch on her belt and wiping at her goggles. "There's nothing like a nice, vigorous ending to an uneventful day."

Chapter 1

Each shift ended with a short but *very* necessary shower to restore herself to something resembling a human being. That was the most inconvenient part of being part of the female staff. There was but one shower to be had, and modesty forbade sharing it with the men; so when the time came for her to wash up, she had to wait until it was unoccupied and post a sign one of the other workers had made for her stating that the showers were RESERVED FOR NITA until she was through. It was one of the reasons she'd switched to the less popular night shift. Regardless of the wait, though, she always hit the shower. Stewing under a layer of marinated leather while she was in the tunnels was all well and good, but it was not a pleasant way to spend one's leisure hours. Now her shift was behind her, her sweat rinsed away, and her dark Calderan skin no longer stained darker by grime and soot. Having changed into her simple white dress, she was ready to go home.

"Good work today, Nita," said the foreman, a man named Stover. "See you tonight?"

"Wouldn't miss it," she said, hanging up her gear in her locker. "I'm going to take a few of the coil boxes, all right?"

Stover gestured vaguely. He was coming off his own shift, and his brain had punched out at the very same moment he had. She likely could have asked if she could borrow his liver and received the same response.

Just inside the walls of the Hub, at the curb of a cobbled street behind a wrought-iron fence, was a clockwork contraption called a "winder." Like so many things in the Hub, it was an accumulation of turning gears and spinning rods, with a grid of metal cubbyholes aligned along the front. Each cubby had a lever at its side, and in the back of the empty ones could be seen a hexagonal socket slowly rotating. Most of the cubbies were small, holding palm-sized boxes, but those nearest to the ground were much larger. She pulled the lever on a pair of the largest occupied cubbies, sliding out a bracket and dispensing two boxes, each three inches thick and a foot square with a matching hexagonal shaft on the front and a handle and switch on top.

"Nita!"

She turned to see one of her fellow night-shift workers, Drew, rushing over to her. He was in his usual after-work outfit—a collared shirt, rough black pants, and beat-up brown shoes—and he carried a large bag of salt on one shoulder and a canvas messenger bag over the other. Since the steamworks generated its energy by piping seawater into boilers warmed by the volcano's heat, an inevitable byproduct was a copious amount of brine, which eventually was allowed to dry in the sun to produce sea salt. Workers were free to take as much as they liked, with the remainder being sold.

"You're looking excited, Drew."

"Why shouldn't I be?" he said, stepping close to add in a conspiratorial whisper, "The airship is coming in tomorrow. I thought I'd swing down and see what they've got to offer. Did I show you what they sold me last time?"

"I don't think so."

He glanced around in a way that did more to make it obvious he was hiding something than it did to keep it hidden, then pulled a leather portfolio from the messenger bag. Nita took it and flipped it open. A passel of thick pieces of paper lay inside, each bearing a grainy black-and-white image. They weren't drawings, or at least not any sort of drawing she had ever seen. As she flipped through them, she came to notice a theme in what the images depicted. They were all pictures of women, each one wearing lacy clothing, and often very little of it.

"Drew, really?" Nita said with a disapproving smirk. "You shouldn't be buying anything from those black marketers from the mainland, and certainly not something as crass as this."

"It isn't crass."

"Oh no?" she asked, plucking out an image of a woman wearing a corset that had nothing to do with supporting her back and everything to do with the more common task of accentuating certain other assets for display.

He snatched the image away and tucked it back into the portfolio, which he then dropped into his bag again. "I was admiring the *fashion*. My sister is a seamstress after all. I thought she might find some inspiration. Besides, have you ever *seen* such things? They call them pho-to-graphs. Apparently you needn't be an artist to create them. They use something called a cam-er-a." He said the unfamiliar words syllable by syllable, as though they were in some alien language. "A push of a button and a puff of smoke, and you've got one of these. If it is *that* easy, I might finally find something of mine hanging in a gallery. I'd need only find the proper things to point the cam-er-a at. I'm hoping they will have one for sale. I imagine there are any number of models who would jump at the chance to be among the first to stand in front of my cam-er-a."

"And no doubt you would ask them to display this wonderful new 'fashion' while they did so?"

"Who knows? One must go where one's muse leads!" He winked at her, then turned to leave. "See you later, Nita."

She waved and carried the coil boxes over to a spindly vehicle near the gate. It looked like a horse-drawn carriage—if someone had been challenged to design one using as little material as possible, and the first thing on the chopping block had been the horse itself. The frame and chassis were little more than thick wire. The wheels were hoops half her height with thin spokes and narrow treads. She opened a container between the rear wheels and slotted one of the coil boxes inside. Once she had flipped the switch on top, she climbed into the seat and twiddled the levers a bit. Gears clicked and spun, and the vehicle rolled quietly into the street, powered by the unwinding spring inside the coil box.

Amanita still lived on the Graus family estate, on the far side of the town nearest to the steamworks. Since the Hub was considered something of an eyesore by the locals, even the closest towns were a fair distance away, but she didn't mind. It gave her a chance each day to take in the scenery of the breathtaking Tellahn countryside. The islands were fortunate enough to enjoy temperate weather through most of the year, and the local flora was lush and tropical. This came at the price of a vicious storm season each year, but that was well behind them for now, and she was free to enjoy the morning breeze and fresh air.

For one who had never visited Caldera, the splendor of even the lesser cities was a sight to behold. Dell Harbor was anything but small and shone as one of the brightest jewels in Tellahn's crown. Even Amanita, who had spent her life here, was frequently struck by the beauty of the place. The Calderans valued inspiration and creation above all else, and it showed in everything they did. Elegant columns and intricate statuary adorned even modest homes. The streetlights were cast and polished with the same care as a set of fine silverware and gleamed in the sun.

She passed through the flowered trellis of her family's tastefully landscaped front garden just as the family was gathering around the breakfast table. As they did every morning, her mother and siblings took their breakfast on the family's sun porch where they could enjoy the sights and aromas of their front garden in the warmth of the rising sun. Amanita quickly took a seat. Already at the table were her fraternal twin sister, Analita, and her younger brother, Joshua. Both were dressed in their pajamas, more accustomed to starting their day with the sunrise than finishing it, as Nita did.

"Late again, Miss Amanita. Trouble at the steamworks?" asked Marissa, the cook. She was a matronly older woman with a frizz of silver hair barely tamed by a white bonnet. In her hand she held a basket of freshly baked rolls, which she added to a table already set with fine china and an assortment of fruits, pastries, and hot cereal.

"Nothing much. A chunk of scale from boiler three broke free and jammed one of the secondary manifolds. The whole thing nearly blew its top, but a few of us managed to release the pressure. Just got a bit messy is all," Nita explained as she buttered herself a roll.

"Nothing much," said her mother, Gloria, with a cluck of her tongue. "It sounds awfully dangerous to me."

The matriarch of the Graus clan, Gloria Graus looked very much the part. Time had done little to fade her beauty over the years. What few lines and wrinkles had found their way into her features served only to underscore her elegance. She fixed her hair, striped with its first strands of silver, pulled back into a tight bun, and even at the breakfast table she wore a gown, petticoat, and satin gloves. There was a telling weariness to her, though, a bone-deep fatigue that was out of place so early in the morning.

"Don't worry so much, Mother. It isn't anything we haven't been trained for. I just had to put the old monkey-toe to use."

"You know, Miss Barken from the art academy was just talking about opening their doors again. I could have your father talk to her about reserving a spot for you."

"Mother, we've been through this..."

"I just feel that you deserve a chance to have a calling in life that is a bit more—"

Nita rolled her eyes and completed the sentence: "Proper? Ladylike? Acceptable?"

"I was going to say artistic."

Amanita's mother had never truly approved of her daughter's decision to take a job at the steamworks. It was only right, in the eyes of most Calderans, to devote one's life to the creation of objects of beauty. No one held this view closer to their hearts than the Graus clan. Over the generations, Nita's family had produced some of the finest sculptors, musicians, and painters in all of Caldera. That tradition continued to this day. Each of Nita's siblings had found a suitably creative calling.

Analita was a dancer and artist's model. Though she shared a birthday with Nita, the pair were anything but identical. Nita, quite lovely in her own right, seemed terribly plain beside Lita. Beside Lita a *goddess* would be plain. Tall and slim with dancer's legs, Lita had a flawless face and a rhythmic grace that showed in her every motion. Her eyes were ice blue, a match for her mother's, and she took the time each morning to paint her fingernails, color her lips, pull up her hair, and otherwise put an artist's touch to her delicate features. Nita wasn't quite as tall, wasn't quite as well proportioned, and wasn't quite as graceful. Her eyes were her father's brown, her hair a deep brown rather than her sister's glorious black. In short, she wasn't quite Lita. In her youth it had been a point of great envy, but such childish feelings had been left behind... for the most part.

Joshua was eighteen years old, two years younger than his sisters. He was the spitting image of his father: a strong, stout build, deep brown eyes, short brown hair, and a head taller than Nita. Though just finishing his schooling, he had already made a name for himself as both a sculptor and a musician. A part of that, perhaps, was having Lita as a model and dancer for his compositions, but his original works earned no less renown. The two of them had become precisely what the rest of Tellahn had expected them to be; fine artists and worthy inheritors of the Graus name.

When Nita became a steamworker, many viewed it as an admission of defeat. Those who found a place in a more utilitarian role weren't precisely looked down upon in Calderan society, but they were universally viewed as those who had failed to find a way to contribute to the beauty of their land. In a way, this was true of Nita. As a child she'd tried her very best to follow in the family tradition. Alas, she didn't have the legs for dance, nor the ear for music. Though her hands were steady enough, she didn't have the eye for painting or sculpture. It wasn't until she tried her hand at constructing the intricate clockwork music boxes that had brought her father his fortune that she found her true talent. She was a tinkerer, and something in the building of a mechanism ignited her passion. Perhaps she could have continued with the clockwork sculptures and music boxes and earned the position her countrymen viewed as her birthright, but what held her fascination wasn't the beauty of the machines, but the way they worked. It was thus only a matter of time before she found her way into the steamworks, the grandest mechanism in all of Caldera.

"You shouldn't have to toil away in that place."

"I *like* to 'toil away in that place,' Mother. I do important work there, and I do it well. Foreman Stover says the system-wide pressure losses have been down four notches since I was made a free-wrench."

Gloria gave her daughter a gentle smile of encouragement that betrayed a complete lack of understanding of anything Nita had said, save that it seemed to be a point of pride. "Well, that's lovely, dear."

"Where is father this morning?" Joshua asked, spooning out a serving of the steamy pot of oatmeal set on the table.

"Your father had to leave early, I'm afraid. He's to discuss matters with the council in Drummer's Valley again today."

"The council? About what?"

"That's your father's business, dear. Something about the perimeter battery, I imagine. No doubt they want to request another contribution to be sure the guns are greased and ready."

"They certainly have been discussing the guns an awful lot lately," Lita said, selecting a peach from the fruit bowl.

"I hear the folks from the west have been making airships that can go even higher. We've got to improve our guns or they might be out of range, now."

"It still seems silly to me," Lita said. "As far as I can remember we've never even *fired* those guns except to test them, and at the annual memorial celebrations. Surely if the outsiders had wanted to invade, they would have done so by now. Better to dismantle the ugly things. Make room for a magnificent lighthouse or two. Or perhaps a really grand statue like they have at the mouth of Meristis Straight. That titan could really use a bride."

"Oh, I'm sure the outsiders would *love* that. You know what a mess the rest of the world is. Foul air. People floating about in those ugly machines. Keeping them out is the only thing that has kept us safe from the same fate," Joshua said. "They are completely lawless out there..."

Nita filled her dish as her brother spouted the same tired speech she'd been hearing her entire life. Caldera had indeed closed its borders to the outside many decades ago, long before she or even her parents were born. These days the only time people were likely to get a glimpse of a foreigner was during one of the few authorized trade visits, or else by sneaking off and trading with black marketers as Drew did. Everything she knew about the outside was based on hearsay and rumor. It was said that their technology was far beyond that of Caldera, with swift airships that could cross the sea in days instead of weeks and mechanisms that made the coil carriage look primitive by comparison. Of course, she'd also heard they were enslaved by a legion of ghoulish fiends and their favorite food was boiled rat. Like most things, Nita took the tales of their exploits with a grain of salt.

"I hear they even throw their own airmen into the sea for the most minor offenses, and..."

"Mother, is something wrong?" Lita said.

Nita looked up to see her mother slowly lowering her teacup to the table. Her hand shook visibly, threatening to spill it.

"It is nothing, dear. Put it out of your mind," she said, rubbing her fingers with her other hand.

"It's getting worse, isn't it?" Nita said.

"It's *nothing*. I... just didn't get very much sleep, dear. I'm tired."

"Have the treatments been helping?" Nita asked.

"Yes, yes, dear, of course. It will pass," she said, holding out her hand as the tremor began to subside. "There, you see? Nothing to worry about."

In her day, Gloria Graus had been the finest sculptor in Caldera, if not the world. Shortly after her children were born, however, she noticed an unsteadiness in her hands. To her and the family's horror, she was found to be suffering Gannt's Disease. It was rare, no more than three cases had been recorded in the history of Caldera, but the prognosis was well-known. Shakiness was just the first symptom, but it had already robbed her of the precision necessary to honor her muse. For a lifelong artist, that was almost worse than the disease's ultimate result: early death. The family tried not to discuss it, as what little could be done had been done. Yet if the tremors were back, it meant the end could be very near.

"Now. Let us not have sour faces around my table, hmm?" said Marissa as she cleared away the emptied dishes. "Josh and Lita have a full day ahead of them, and Nita has a long day behind her."

"Yes, off with you, children. The academy wants me to select a lecturer to fill in for me."

The family stood to go about their day, but Nita lingered. Her mother had moved unsteadily to the parlor and stood staring at something on the mantle. It was littered with vases, statues, sketches, and paintings, as well as a large handmade clock of Nita's father's design. Gloria could have been staring at any one of them, but Nita knew without asking which it was that held her mother's gaze.

"Mother?"

"Oh. Yes, Amanita dear?" she answered, shaken from her reverie.

"How long has it been?" Nita asked, plucking a small figurine of a deer from the mantle. It was skillfully made from clay, but, unlike the other figurines, it was unglazed and unpainted.

"Oh… sixteen years now. Oh cruel fate, eh? To take my gift from me before I could paint my final piece." She paused to settle down to a chair. These days she couldn't spend more than a few minutes on her feet. "Tell me, dear. What you do at the steamworks, does it make you happy? Does it feed your spirit and nourish your heart?"

"It is very fulfilling."

"Then cherish it, love. You won't have it forever. And you never know when you might lose it. I think back sometimes. To balls I attended, galas I hosted. I think of all the hours I could have spent with my fingers in the clay or with a chisel in my hand. There isn't anything I wouldn't give to have just one of those hours back again. Just one more day that I could hold a brush and know that the line I paint would stay straight and true." A tear ran down her cheek. "Oh, but listen to me. No sense talking like that. We look to the future in this family. I can still teach, eh? Off with you. Get some rest. Don't listen to your silly old mother."

Nita lingered for a moment more, looking thoughtfully at the unfinished figurine, then placed it on the mantle and left her mother to rest.

Chapter 2

That evening, as the sun was setting, Nita arrived at the steamworks for her shift. The events of the morning were still heavy on her mind, but she tried to push them aside and focus on the task at hand. The day shift had removed the broken section of pipe and the jammed valve, but daylight had run out before the replacement could be installed, leaving it for Nita and her partner to do. Tonight that partner happened to be Drew.

"Blast it," he muttered to himself. "I must have left my five-sixteenths in the locker. Do you have yours?"

Nita slipped a wrench from her tool sash. "You really ought to take better care of your tools."

"Yeah, yeah. Give me a break; I've got other things on my mind today."

"Oh, that's right. Your picture device. You know, trading with the outsiders is strictly enforced and very limited. I don't think we've had a legitimate shipment in three years. How exactly do you plan to get away with using this device if you manage to buy one?"

"I'll just say I found it in a curio shop from the old days before we closed the borders. For all anyone knows, the cam-er-a is an ancient invention out there. Heaven knows they come up with some remarkable gadgets. And *fine* spirits, too. We make better wine, but the whiskey from out there? Hits you like a *hammer*."

Nita raised the new valve into place and steadied it while Drew began to tighten the bolts.

"Do they have anything besides pointless toys and things to feed your vices?"

"Possibly. Once they pulled out the liquor I stopped paying attention to anything else."

Nita narrowed her eyes.

"Relax, Nita. I kid. They have all sorts of things. They make excellent optics. My best telescope came from them. They're always eager to show off their firearms as well, but even *I'm* not foolish enough to be caught with one of those. There are rare delicacies, exotic fabrics and pelts, tinctures, ointments..."

"They sell medicines?"

"Well, I wouldn't call them *medicines*. One was to regrow hair. Another was to, er, restore vigor."

"Oh. Well, do they work?"

"What are you implying?" he asked, nervously running his fingers through his hair and checking his reflection in the fresh pipe section.

"You know what I mean."

"If you're so interested, why don't you come along? We'll take my brother's boat up to Moor Spires. They're due to dock there in a few hours. They'll be leaving just before morning, so hopefully this replacement doesn't take all night, and we can skip out a bit early."

"Well… no. I didn't bring any money."

"No need. They don't have any use for our currency. Why would they? Fortunately for us, it is just as difficult for them to get Calderan goods as it is for us to get theirs. Sea salt, jewelry, anything we make is worth more than gold to them. If you *really* want to get in their good graces, bring them something made of trith."

"Trith? The stuff they make the coils from?"

He nodded. "They can't make it out there. They'll trade just about anything to get some."

Another gift from the volcano, trith was first created centuries before by some of the very first settlers on the islands. An alloy made of half a dozen metals and a special mineral found only in the volcanic stone of the mountains, it had properties that no other metal could match. Paper-thin ribbons of the stuff could be made into coil springs that could store ten times the energy of a steel one, seemingly without fatigue. Thin bars of the stuff were stronger than several inches of iron, and once forged not even the heart of Tellahn's volcano could manage to do much more than soften it. It didn't rust or even tarnish. It was little surprise that its creators named it trith, which, in the old tongue, meant perfection. The formula for creating it existed as a closely guarded secret, and making it proved quite expensive, but it was nonetheless common in Caldera thanks to the fact that nearly all that had ever been made was still in use.

Perhaps seeing her will weakening, Drew pressed on. "Come on, if nothing else you'll get a chance to meet someone from outside of Caldera. Not many who can say they've done that."

She turned the offer over in her head. It would be a lie to say she'd never been curious about things beyond the Calderan borders. One of the few regrets she had about working in the steamworks was the simple fact that her skills would be of use in few places on the isles, and thus there would never likely be anything new or exciting to look forward to in her career. A small but vocal part of her yearned for novelty, to see new sights and experience new things. If nothing else, these black-market folks promised plenty to see.

"All right. I'll join you this time. But neither of us are going anywhere if we don't get this valve in."

Few better ways exist to ensure problems will arise in a given task than by making plans for afterward. Halfway through completing the installation they discovered that one of the mounting holes hadn't been machined properly. Once it had been removed, corrected, and fitted again, the supply crew managed to send along the wrong size nuts and bolts. The horizon was already starting to get rosy when they finally finished up the project and were given permission to leave.

"Ugh, I feel disgusting," she said, hurrying out of the last roughly hewn tunnel and into the locker room.

"Well, you'll have to feel disgusting a bit longer if you want to make it to the market on time. We've got to leave now, no time to shower," Drew warned. He checked the clock and quickly emptied his locker into a bag.

"I suppose I can bring my clothes and get changed when I go home. We'll be done before the sun is up; there shouldn't be *too* many people to offend with my ripeness."

"And just think of the wonders you'll be bringing with you! Which reminds me. Don't forget to bring something to trade."

She nodded and hastily grabbed a few bags of salt and a brooch she'd left in her locker months ago. After a moment of thought, she grabbed a large coil box and two smaller ones. The prospective payments were loaded into a bag and thrown over her shoulder. With that they made their way quickly to the pier a few streets away, where Drew's brother Linus waited in the early morning fog.

The boat was anything but impressive, a simple, flat skiff. It had two large paddlewheels on the side for propelling and steering, and a sputtering boiler to power them occupied the rear. Being a Calderan vessel, however, it was painted with bright, cheery colors in an intricate scheme and had a figurehead carved with skill to resemble a barracuda. The side proudly proclaimed it to be *The Triumph.*

"Any later and I'd have left without you," Linus said, flipping open a pocket watch and leaning close to the yellow flame of the boat's oil lamp.

"You'd have wasted your time then, because you don't know today's password. Now let's get on with it before we miss them."

Linus untied the boat, and the trio made their way along the shore to the western side of Tellahn. Their destination was a jagged cluster of outcroppings a bit more than a mile off shore. They were far too small and too steep to be considered islands, standing out of the water like menhirs erected by a particularly haphazard ancient civilization. In the days before Caldera had isolated itself, the cluster served as a neutral ground where authorities could make sure that nothing too dangerous was brought to the islands. Now it was a largely forgotten feature of the shore that just so happened to be perfect for mooring an airship near enough to the surface to avoid drawing too much attention.

The fog turned anything more than a hundred yards out into a shadowy gray form, so it wasn't until they were nearly upon Moor Spires that they saw the airship emerge from the haze. It was lashed to the three tallest stones, and Nita's eyes opened wide at each new detail as it was revealed. Until now, an airship had only ever been a dot in the sky drifting slowly along as it gave her homeland a wide berth. Seeing one up close fascinated her, though even to her untrained eye it was clear that this ship was not what one might call a fine specimen. A bulging, barely intact gas sack comprised the bulk of the vehicle. It had at one point been red, but time and misuse had turned it into a quilt of differently colored patches and grafts. The sack was enormous, perhaps seventy-five feet long and bulging to thirty feet in diameter at its thickest. It was rounded at the front and pointed at the back where a trio of fins stuck off the top and sides, giving it a stretched-out teardrop shape. The thickest part of the sack was wrapped in a wide metal lattice, which served as the mounting point for five barrel-sized nacelles, evenly spaced. Each nacelle was filled with a blossom of short overlapping blades and had a smooth metal cowling.

The hull of the ship dangled below the sack, stretching to forty feet in length and trailing back from the front end of the sack, following a slightly narrower profile. Like the sack, it had signs of obvious patching, strips of blond, unstained wood standing out against the rich brown of the original planks. The overall structure of the ship put one in mind of a yacht-sized pirate ship that had been hauled out of the sea. It had a flat deck on top, separated into a main deck and an elevated tier toward the front to better follow the lower curve of the sack. Below the railing at the edge of the deck was a row of glass and brass portholes running the length of the ship, and below those were a second and third row. Jutting to the left and right from the front of the ship was a pair of cannon clusters, three each, with a single cluster sticking out of the back. Where it departed from the pirate ship motif was the piping, which jutted out of and into the hull with little rhyme or reason, and here and there escaping steam hissed and spat. Black smoke huffed out the back of the ship from three soot-covered metal chimneys. Thick black rubber hoses ran up a wooden runner from the deck to the central band of the sack, leading one by one to the nacelles.

Directly below the ship, a small dinghy hung attached to it by a pair of slackened chains. In the dinghy was a mound of sacks and chests and a young man, who, in the process of relieving himself off the opposite side, had his back to the approaching skiff. The man whistled to himself and, based on the trajectory, was attempting to amuse himself by creating as high an arc as possible. Linus gave the steam whistle a quick pull, startling the young man into what was nearly a messy conclusion to his little interlude.

"Well, that wasn't a very neighborly thing to do to a fella!" called out the young man once he'd managed to finish up and make himself decent again.

"Just wanted to give you a little warning. There's a lady on board today," Linus said.

"Is there? Well, ain't my face red! How do you do, ma'am! I hope you don't mind if I wait until you all are a mite closer before I introduce myself proper, just so's I don't have to yell quite so much."

There was an odd twang to the man's voice, but an earnest quality to his words. He also had a peculiar manner of dressing, at least from Nita's point of view. In Caldera, unless one's occupation dictated otherwise, a certain formality applied to even the most basic outfits. Clothes were tailored, carefully selected, and properly displayed, but no sign of similar care stood out in this man's ensemble. His pants were of a black canvas, faded to gray at the knees. He wore a long brown coat, the sleeves rolled to his elbows, revealing a tan shirt with long sleeves that were similarly rolled. The coat was open, and beneath it was a black vest and a loose-fitting belt weighted heavily down on one side. Now and again a gust of wind pushed the coat open enough to reveal a pistol. The man himself was rail thin, with sandy-blond hair cropped short and a face with a few days of stubble. He had a friendly but incomplete smile and more than a few scars on both his hands and face. Compared to the dark skin of most native Calderans, his skin was very fair, though the sun had baked it a bit brown.

The Triumph pulled close to his little dinghy and threw across ropes to tether them together.

"I apologize for what you seen me do, ma'am. Sun's nearly up and all, which is our cue to skedaddle most days, so I didn't see no harm in heeding to nature's call. Figures you all would show up and make a fool out of ol' Ichabod. That'd be me, by the way, ma'am. Ichabod Cooper. Pleased as punch to meet you." He held tight to the dangling chain and leaned out over the water, extending a hand for a shake.

Nita obliged him. "Amanita Graus."

"Pleasure, Miss Graus. Now, before we get to business, I got to get this out of the way." He reached into a pocket inside his coat and pulled a rough sheet of paper out, staring at what was written upon it as though it was a particularly challenging puzzle to unravel. When he spoke, it was with the slow and unnatural diction of someone who was unaccustomed to reading in general, and completely unused to doing so aloud. "Hel-lo. Dear. Sir. ... Do. You. Have. The. Time."

"The time is bright and early," Drew recited.

Ichabod furrowed his brow, then turned his face upward and bellowed. "That right, Cap'n?"

"Just get on with it," rumbled a reply from somewhere inside the ship.

"Well, all right. So, what are we after today?" Cooper asked. He rubbed his hands together and flipped open some of the chests. "Gunner said you were interested in the girlie pictures last time." He pulled out another portfolio. "We've got some more of those."

Drew cleared his throat in embarrassment. "I was interested in the *fashion.*"

"Oh." Cooper flipped through the portfolio. "Then you probably won't like these. No fashion as such."

"Oh, uh, not so quickly," Drew said as Cooper began to tuck the portfolio away again. "There's an inherent artistic beauty to the female form. I'll trade you a quarter bag of Calderan sea salt for it."

"Sold. Anything else I can do you for today?"

"Last month I'd asked about that device for making these pho-to-graphs."

"Oh, that's right. Gunner said something about that. You're in luck. It took some doing, but we managed to get our hands on one for you." He unearthed a leather-wrapped box with an odd, pleated sleeve emerging from the front. The front of the sleeve was affixed to a lens and mounted to a runner. Knobs and buttons littered the top of the box. "As I understand it, this here box, along with some fancy paper and some bottles of fancy chemicals, are all you need to make them pictures, so long as you follow the instructions. You get the box and enough paper and chemicals for a hundred pictures or so. What's your offer?"

"I'll give you a half bag of salt."

"If we're talking salt, I figure three bags is more in line with the cap'n's expectations."

"I'll go as high as a full bag."

"Then you'll be getting your picture box from someone else."

"Fine, a bag and a half."

Cooper tipped his head from side to side, then quietly said, "I'm not so good with figurin'. How's that compare to three?"

"Favorably," Drew said.

"It's half as much," Nita clarified.

"Eh, half'll do. It's a pain lugging it up and down. Anything else?"

"Just a bottle of whiskey. Ten year."

"The man's got some fine taste. I keep a bottle of this myself, for toothaches and such like." He fished out a stout bottle of thick brown glass. "Let's see. That was a bag and a half for the picture box and all that, plus a quarter bag for the girly pictures. What's say we just call the whole lot of it two bags, so's I don't have to go pouring things out?"

"Suits me," Drew said, hefting the two bags across and receiving his goods in exchange.

"Now, for the lady. What'll it be, ma'am?"

"Do you carry medicines?" Nita asked.

"Oh, we got all sorts of treatments that'll cure your many ills. This here liniment, for instance, is guaranteed to take care of any muscle aches you might have." Cooper revealed a familiar brown bottle.

"That just looks like more whiskey."

"It's got a million uses, ma'am. Treats just about anything that might ail you, particularly if you suffer from what Cap'n calls an 'excess of sobriety,' which I'm sorry to say he's been having quite a bout with of late."

"I was hoping you might have a treatment for a specific disease. Something called Gannt's Disease."

"We mostly carry sundry and recreational-type things. Proper drugs are a bit of a chore to get."

"Well, do you at least know if such a treatment exists?"

"I don't rightly know. I'll check." He looked up and bellowed, "Cap'n! You ever heard of something called… what was it, ma'am?"

"Gannt's Disease," she replied, loudly enough for the unseen captain to hear.

"Well now, a question of a medical nature would more properly be addressed to our resident medical *practitioner*, wouldn't it?" growled the muffled voice.

"Good thinking, Cap'n. Butch! You ever heard of—?"

Before he could finish, a torrent of words in an unrecognizable dialect poured out of a different part of the ship. Cooper nodded thoughtfully.

"Gives you shaky fingers? Makes you keel over after about twenty years or so?" he asked.

Nita nodded, trying to shrug off the casual way in which her mother's plight was described.

"Sounds like it!" Cooper said. More unrecognizable yelling followed. "Seems they don't call it that in our parts. Them fuggers got that one worked out, though. Not the sort of thing they'd usually share with the likes of us, though."

"Fuggers? Wait, are you telling me there is a cure?"

"Butch seems to think so, but like I said, we don't carry it. It'd be a fair bit of trouble to lay our hands on some."

"I don't care. I'll pay any price."

"For a special order like that, it'd be a pretty big price, ma'am."

"I am Amanita Graus, one of the oldest daughters of the Graus clan. We are among the most wealthy and influential families in all of Caldera. I can meet any price."

Cooper looked her up and down and gave the air a sniff. "I don't pretend to know how rich folk from your parts usually look or smell, but I gotta say, you ain't what comes to mind. Not that it matters, of course.

Round these parts, cachet don't mean too much. You're only as rich as what you brung with you. So how much you got?"

"I've got three bags of salt."

"A special order like that? Three bags is a good start, but it won't get you all the way there. What else you got?"

She rummaged through her bag and revealed the brooch. It was polished silver, engraved with complex filigree, and set with amethyst and amber. By Calderan standards it was quaint and simple. Judging from how wide Cooper's eyes had grown, he had a higher opinion of it.

"Cap'n! She's got a bit of jewelry here that I think'll pay for... well, I think it's... remember back when we had to replace some turbines and you had to sell that ring of yours? It's about like that."

"That'll do," the captain hollered back.

"Right, ma'am. We'll take the salt and the jewelry and head on out to see if we can't find that medicine of yours. We'll be back just about this time next month. The pass phrase is—"

"Oh no. I'm not giving you this payment just to send you off with the hopes of getting what I paid for. I want some sort of guarantee."

"There ain't no guarantee to be *had*, ma'am. The fuggers ain't too keen on parting with stuff like that. We'll have to meet with our supplier. There'll be discussions, haggling and such. Might be we'll be back again next month with empty hands. Of course, we'll give you your payment back, minus some expenses, but—"

"Then I'm coming with you."

"Ma'am, you can ask your friend. We ain't gonna just run off with your money. We're professional."

"It is non-negotiable."

"We ain't no passenger liner, ma'am."

"I'll pay extra, but this is very important to me, and if there are negotiations to be done, I want to be present to see that everything in your power is being done to attain the treatment."

"I understand, ma'am, but there's more to it than that," he said, vague frustration behind the words, as though he was running through a tiresome and all-too-frequent speech. "Smuggling a few odds and ends back and forth is one thing. Doing the same with people on board looks an awful lot worse to the people who might catch us. You'll be with us for a month. If people get the idea we took you without your permission, that's kidnapping or trafficking or some such. Not to mention you might die, which your folks might call war. That'd cost us pretty dear. Ain't worth the risk."

"If it will cost you more, then I'll pay more. I've got this."

She revealed one of the smaller coil boxes. Upon seeing it, Drew's eyes shot open and he snatched the box from her hand.

"Are you crazy?" he said.

"What? You said they liked trith."

"Did you say trith?" Cooper said, interest piqued.

"I said a *bit* of trith. A few washers or something. Not a whole coil box."

"How much you got there, ma'am?"

She snatched it back from Drew and slipped a screwdriver from her tool sash. A few deft twists loosened the face plate, which she twisted aside to reveal the purple-black spiral within. She handed the box across to Cooper. He took it, then fished in his pocket until he found a coin. Clutching the box tight in his hand, he scratched the coin against the coil, then held it up to find a neat little notch had been carved out of the coin without so much as a scratch on the coil.

"Uh, Cap'n!" he said, his voice a bit shaky. "This young lady here wants to ride along while we look for her medicine for her."

"Well, then you explain our policy regarding passengers."

"I did. She's willing to pay with trith. Got a whole box here. Feels like about half a pound."

"And there's more where that came from," Nita said, loudly enough to be overheard.

The waves lapped against the boats as all waited for an answer.

"Did you tell her the *whole* passenger policy?"

"Oh, right. Forgot that other bit." He turned to Nita. "You reckon you'll be able to pitch in and all that?"

"I'll do my best."

"That ain't the question, ma'am. We all do our best. The question is, do you reckon your best will be good enough to do the job? And to pay the consequences if you don't measure up?"

"I'll do whatever it takes."

He looked her up and down. "She looks like she might be able to lend a decent hand along the way, and she says she's willing. What do you say, Cap'n? … Cap'n?"

After a short pause, the splash of a rope ladder unfurling into the water between the boats came as the captain's answer.

"Well, all right then." He handed back the coil box and held out a hand to help her over. "Welcome aboard the *Wind Breaker*, ma'am."

"Nita, you can't do this," said Drew.

"If it means giving mother her life back, or at least her life's calling for even a few years, then I must."

Cooper gave two quick tugs to the chain. “Get ready to haul the captain’s gig once we’re up! We’re running late as it is! Watch yourself, ma’am. After you.”

Nita tested the strength of thc ladder, then slipped the coil box into a pouch on her belt, strapped her bag to her back, and began to climb.

“You’ve got the passwords for next month, right, Drew?” Cooper said.

“Yeah, I do. Nita, think about this for a moment. It will be dangerous out there! You’re breaking the law! We’re not supposed to leave the borders of Caldera without permits! What’ll I tell the foreman? What’ll I tell your mother?”

“Tell them I went on a trip. I haven’t taken any leave in months,” she called over her shoulder. “I’ll be fine, Drew. How bad could it be?”

Chapter 3

Nita, still heavily loaded with her tools and the sack that contained her payment and her change of clothes, labored a bit to reach the top of the shaky ladder. Things became slightly easier once the bottom of the ladder pulled taut with a second passenger, but after a moment a realization came to mind.

"Mr. Cooper?" she called over her shoulder.

"You can call me Coop, ma'am," he replied.

"Very well, Coop," she said, stopping for a moment to catch her breath and better engage in conversation. "Are you staring at my bottom right now?"

"Well, ma'am, you're ahead of me on the ladder. I can't rightly do otherwise at present," he said. "I was always taught ladies first, but I don't think Ma and Pa ever anticipated this particular situation. Could be worse though, ma'am. At least you're wearing britches instead of a skirt."

"True enough. I don't suppose you could look aside until I reach the top of the ladder."

"If it'd make you more comfortable, ma'am, but if its privacy you're looking for, you'll find it a bit hard to find on an airship. Close quarters and cramped spaces don't leave too much room for modesty, and thing's'll be a good deal tighter with another soul on board. Looking away now, ma'am."

"Thank you, Coop."

She hurried up the final stretch of ladder and crawled through a small hatch in the belly of the ship. It was wrapped in three sides by a railing and led into a tight, dim little room that smelled strongly of gear oil and burning coal. The roof was low, barely high enough for her to stand without stooping, and the only light came from a handful of bizarre little contraptions arranged along the top edge of the wall. They looked like glass pipes with brass fittings on either end, and they gave off a weakly pulsing glow of sickly yellow-green. At either end of the room was a winch, and manning the lever beside one of them waited a young woman with more than a passing resemblance to Cooper, who was pulling himself into the ship now. In the center of the room was a much larger hatch than the one they'd climbed through, beneath which hung the boat.

"Haul it up. I'll pull in the mooring lines, and we can skedaddle before the fog breaks up and the Calderan scouts notice us. Once we're clear I'll hop down and hand up the goods," Cooper said. He was tall enough that he had to slouch a bit to avoid scraping his head, but he did so with a practiced ease that didn't cost him any speed. "Oh, and this here's Amanita Graus. She'll be joining us for a bit."

"I know who she is. You think I couldn't hear you jawing back and forth?" said the woman as Coop hurried off. She pulled the lever, prompting a hiss that brought the winches to life, then extended a hand. "Pleased to meet you, Amanita. Did I hear your friend down there calling you Nita?"

"Yes. Most people call me that. Amanita can be a mouthful at times."

"Nita it is, then. I'm Chastity. Folks round here call me Lil. Short for Lil' Coop, seein' as how I'm Coop's baby sister."

"A pleasure to meet you."

"The cap'n will want to meet you before anyone else. He'll be at the helm on the main deck, so we'll just head up there when the gig is reeled in."

Nita stood, looking down through the larger hatch and listening to the click of the winch. As she did, two very distinct and very powerful feelings came over her. The first was an intense feeling of vertigo. The climb hadn't seemed terribly long when she was looking up, but looking down was another matter. The waves below made her head spin, and realizing that they were held aloft not by something good and solid like a building but by a tattered bag and some ancient rigging filled her with a cold, hollow anxiety.

The second feeling, one easily as unsettling, was the realization of just what she had done and how quickly she had done it. Everything had happened so fast! In the space of a few minutes the distant hope of a treatment for her mother's problem had turned into an opportunity that could easily slip away. In the moment, her decision seemed like the only one. There hadn't been time for fear or doubt. In a way it was just the same as the day before when she'd raced to the bypass valve. Had she thought about it, running *toward* a boiler that was on the verge of explosion was a hideously stupid idea, but in the end it had been the right thing to do. She could only hope that this decision was the right one, too. In these first moments after stepping off the proverbial cliff, it certainly didn't seem that way.

After one last glance through the hatch, she swallowed hard and hastily decided not to think about any more cliffs for a while, proverbial or otherwise.

The hoisted dinghy finally drew near enough to the hatch to completely block her view of the water below, and Lil threw the lever in the opposite direction.

"That'll do 'er for now. Let's get you up to meet the cap'n before—"

A brass pipe with a flared opening ran from the wall to the ceiling, and from it blared a gruff and distorted voice. "Lil, get our passenger to the deck."

"You can set your watch by that man," she whispered irritably. She stepped up to the flared end and spoke into it. "On our way, Cap'n."

Lil motioned for Nita to follow, then ducked through the low doorway. Nita took a moment to push her worrying attitude and more worrying circumstances out of her mind and tried to busy it with other tasks, like taking in her new surroundings and shipmates. Lil was dressed much as her brother was, minus the long coat and with the addition of a tattered red bow holding what was probably shoulder-length hair into a short ponytail. Her boots had a more pronounced heel, and she had on worn leather fingerless gloves. Grease, soot, and one or two other things Nita couldn't identify smudged her clothes and face. All things considered, she could easily have passed for one of the workers in the steamworks.

She led Nita through a series of short and horribly cramped hallways. Though there were plenty of doorways, there were very few doors. Curtains seemed to be the norm where privacy was called for, and elsewhere even *they* were absent. Each room was claustrophobic and had every square inch of space crammed with maps, tools, or boxes. Space, it would seem, was at a premium here, so much so that much of the infrastructure and workings of the ship were entirely exposed. Pipes crisscrossed the ceiling, and tubes ran in sagging bundles laced between them. Here and there they would poke up to the next level or down through the floor, and valves and gauges seemed to be randomly scattered about their lengths. Again, it was not unlike the chaos she worked in every day at the steamworks, albeit in miniature. Having so much copper and brass around her made her feel a bit more at ease, like seeing a familiar face in a strange town.

Lil led the way to a ladder that brought them three decks up, where it emerged onto the open top of the ship. For a moment, any doubt she had was wiped away by pure fascination. The very top of one of the lower spires was at eye level here, giving her a point of reference of not only how high they were, but how much they were swaying with each breeze. Coop and another man were busy along the railing at the edge of the deck, tugging at small ropes to untie large ones. She could hear the peculiar fans turning above her, a regular pattern of squeaks, rattles, and hisses forming a sort of rhythm to which the deck crew worked.

"You're gonna want to hang onto something," Lil said. "Coop's just about got the last line loose, and then comes the big swing."

Nita steadied herself against one of the support struts that ran up to the gas bladder, and not a moment too soon. When a mooring line came loose, the whole of the vessel lurched away from it, swinging like a pendulum. The fans rattled to life, righting the ship against the remaining line, which the other deck worker released a moment later, prompting a second and far more ponderous swing. The tempo of the fans quickened into a steady buzz, and the ropes above her creaked and whined with the ship's acceleration. Stone spires passed by near enough to spit on, and then the world around them pitched hard to the side as the airship took a sharp turn. Nita's knees almost gave out when she turned to the left and received an unobscured view of the ocean, the angle of the deck so sharp that she felt sure she and everyone else should be tumbling off.

The turn tapered off and the ship righted itself, but Nita was reluctant to release her grip. Everything around her still seemed to pitch and roll in a stomach-turning way. Lil continued toward the steps leading up to the upper tier, then turned when she realized Nita wasn't following her.

"Come on, the cap'n's up at the fore end. What are you waiting for?"

"I'm waiting for the ship to settle a bit," Nita said, deciding to leave out the bit about waiting for her stomach to do the same.

Lil smirked. "Ship's as settled as it's gonna get until we're tied to something solid again. You'll get used to it pretty quick if you stick around long enough. Or you'll go overboard," she added with a shrug. "Believe it or not, I fell over once, on my first launch. No one warned me about the swing. Wasn't the sort of thing I wanted to happen twice, so I got my air legs right quick after that. Come on, this way."

Lil led the way, and Nita stumbled behind her like a drunk until they reached the front end of the ship, where the captain stood at something that looked like a cross between a traditional ship's helm and the control harness for one of the steam drills they used to excavate new rooms in the steamworks back home. A spoked control wheel rose from the deck in front of him, and beside him trailed a row of brass levers with linkages between them such that no lever could move too far along without dragging its neighbors with it. The levers had ancient, tarnished labels riveted to a weathered wooden control board. Those that she could read said things like "Turbine 3" or "Forward, 1/4 power" with graduated markings indicating further fractions of power. Tubes, ropes, and chains led in a tangled knot both up and down from the controls, leading to pulleys and manifolds that distributed adjustments all around the ship. The captain's hand danced across them, sliding this lever up and twisting that knob while making minor adjustments to the wheel. Opposite the panel of levers and knobs stood a second panel outfitted with compasses, spinning wind meters, and other instruments.

After marveling at the apparatus responsible for running the ship, Nita took a moment to observe the man. Dressed similarly to the rest of the crewmembers she'd seen, his clothing suggested that it may have been some sort of uniform, but he clearly wore it with more care and pride. The sleeves of his long coat weren't rolled. He wore it open, like the others, flapping in the breeze. His vest was straight and buttoned, a gold chain leading from a buttonhole to his watch pocket. His trousers were black, but less worn than those of his crew, and his boots were polished to a higher sheen and were of a much finer make. He wore thin tan gloves with openings over the knuckles and between the fingers. Around his head he'd tied a charcoal-gray kerchief, and a pair of round spectacles with dark glass lenses and a strange rectangular side lens stretching back from the hinge to shade his eyes from the side adorned his face. Long steel-gray hair hung down from beneath the kerchief, and he wore a similarly colored beard and mustache, which looked to have been carefully trimmed at some point in the past but had since been neglected. He was perhaps in his fifties, though his skin was weathered, roasted, and pitted enough to make him seem far older. His teeth, whiter than she'd expected, clamped around the smoldering stub of a thin brown cigar that burned with an almost candylike scent. While his crew so far had all run on the thin side, he was overall thicker and more intimidating, not portly or muscle-bound, just broader in his chest, arms, and legs.

"Cap'n Mack, Amanita Graus. Nita, this is Cap'n Mack," Lil said.

The captain turned to Nita and gave her a measuring look. "Let's see the trith." He spoke out of the side of his mouth rather than sparing a hand for long enough to take the cigar away, and his voice was rough enough to make it clear that this wasn't his first cigar. It probably wasn't even in the first thousand.

She pulled the exposed coil box out of its pouch and held it out to him. He glanced down to it, then back to her eyes, not a flicker of a change in his expression to suggest what might be going through his mind. When he held out his hand, she placed the box in it.

The captain inspected it for few moments. "Gunner, get over here and take the wheel. Lil, go handle packing up the mooring lines. Ms. Graus, this way please," said the captain. Despite the presence of the word "please," all three statements were clearly orders.

The crew snapped to his commands, and he strode quickly toward the steps down from the upper tier without waiting for an answer from Nita. In her years at the steamworks, she'd worked under enough different foremen and supervisors to know that it didn't do you any good to illustrate an inability to follow directions as a first impression. She didn't know enough about this captain to know what kind of man he was, so it was best to stay on his good side. He walked along the swaying deck with nary a stutter or a stumble, as though he didn't even notice the way it pitched and rolled with the breeze. Nita didn't even try to follow him directly, resorting instead to the same roundabout path that she'd taken to reach him, one that gave her uninterrupted contact with a railing or strut.

Nita reached the stairs and found the captain standing in a doorway at the bottom of another staircase, this one leading back toward the top tier of the deck and providing access to the ship's interior beneath it. When she caught up with him, he turned and led her down a short hallway to a door emblazoned with a plaque that read CAPTAIN'S QUARTERS. The captain pushed open the door to what Nita expected to be the grandest room on the ship. Though they had no airships, Caldera had glorious and well-appointed seagoing vessels. As a Graus she'd often been offered a place at the captain's table during mealtimes and had been given the ship's tour on the flagship of the Calderan fleet. On each of those ships the captain's quarters had been a place large enough and comfortable enough to match a room one might find on solid land.

This was not a policy shared by the captain of the *Wind Breaker*. The captain's quarters were as cramped as any other room she'd seen, if not more so. It contained a desk piled with maps, books, and manifests, all held in place by leather straps affixed to the desk's corners. The walls were entirely covered with built-in shelving and cabinets, and most bulged with bottles, boxes, and more papers. The opposite wall had three large portholes, and strung across the space in front of them was a net hammock. Nita took a deep breath and immediately regretted it, as the very wood of this room was saturated with the same sickly sweet smell as the cigar in his mouth, though there were a few earthy undertones that put one in mind of a barnyard. A map of the world was pinned to the ceiling, with Caldera among a handful of locations marked. A pair of chairs occupied the remaining floor space, one behind the desk and one in front of it.

"Take a seat," he said, doing the same as he placed the coil box on the desk. He pulled at drawers on his side of the desk, revealing first a tall, narrow jar with a locking top, from which he pulled a cigar. From another drawer he extracted a box of matches and a tin box, into which he placed what remained of his cigar stub. He struck the match, lit the cigar with care, and drew in a long breath, which he released with a few smoky words. "What's your game, Ms. Graus?"

She waved off the cloud of smoke that carried his words and coughed a bit. "Game, Captain? I thought I'd been quite clear about my intentions."

"A pretty young girl from a well-to-do family kicks up a fuss and buys herself onto my rust bucket of a ship for a king's ransom and for darn near no real reason. All that after a couple of generations of no one having a mind to so much as go sightseeing off those islands of yours. Either you're up to something, or you're not quite right in the head. Could be a bit of both, I reckon."

"My mother suffers from Gannt's Disease, and we've no way to treat it properly. At worst she could be weeks from death; at best the treatments will preserve her for a few years more. She is a young woman, Captain, no older than you. If there is even the smallest chance to cure her, I don't know that there is any other choice to make."

"Even if you're speaking the God's honest truth, I don't think you've thought this through."

"I'll admit I tend to be a bit impulsive when things look desperate, but the choices I make tend to be the correct ones. I stand by what I've said. I don't know that a person in my position could have, in good conscience, acted any differently."

"Don't you, now? Well, let's see how a man in *my* position ought to act. This is all idle musing, mind you. Just for the sake of for instance and such. Here's the way I see it. I run a floating black market, so I'm clearly not an angel. A wealthy heiress falls into my lap. Seems to me like a nice healthy ransom would be in order."

Nita stiffened in her seat.

"Most of the folk in my line wouldn't think twice about it. Hell, if I were ten years younger, I might have tried it myself, but those guns round the border would make it a mite tricky to deliver the demand, and I'm just not up to the effort. No, ma'am, ransom isn't what I've got in mind. The easiest thing to do would be to kill you, keep what's worth keeping from that bag of yours, and heave the rest in the sea, you along with it." He picked up the coil box. "This here? A lot of men have spilled a lot of blood for a lot less, and as I understand it, this isn't the half of it. You want my honest opinion, Ms. Graus? I don't see a lot of ways this comes out right for you. What's to keep me from just picking these boxes apart and not giving your medicine no never mind?"

She took a slow breath. "Well, Captain, and again for the sake of 'for instance' as you put it, if you were to try pulling one of these apart, I don't think you'd be doing much else ever again. I've seen these boxes being built. I apprenticed under their maker, in fact. It takes a hell of a lot of force to get that trith coiled. If you give it the chance to uncoil without the proper care, it will straighten itself out, and something that thin moving that fast won't slow down much on its way through wood, steel, flesh, or bone. In case you haven't noticed, those cross pieces holding that box together are *also* made of trith, because anything less couldn't withstand the stress. Once I'm satisfied you've done all you can to keep your end of the bargain, I'll be happy to show you how to take one apart and maybe even help you cut it up. But not before."

"And if I decide to sell it intact?"

Nita sat quietly, trying to keep her expression steady and hoping that it came across as steely resolve rather than panicked realization. The captain let the silence hang in the air for an uncomfortably long time before he saw fit to break it.

"Don't worry yourself, miss. I did a fair amount of mischief in my younger days, but I haven't got the vinegar for that anymore. Better or worse, I'm a businessman now, and I pride myself as a straight shooter. It's cost me a fortune, I reckon. Plenty of men I could have swindled good, if I'd had the mind to. But being honest also kept my head off of the chopping block and out of the noose more than once. I'll take that trade ten times out of ten. Heavy pockets don't do much more than weigh you down when you're swinging from the gallows. Far as I'm concerned, we've got a deal." He puffed the cigar once more. "But I want to make sure you understand what sort of a deal it is. First, tide's got to be pretty low for us to make use of those mooring stones, and it's got to happen at night, so we only make stops in your neck of the woods roundabout once a month, if we can manage. That's how long you'll be with us, at the very least. Acceptable?"

"If that's what it takes."

"And things won't be easy. I ain't made a single trip between Caldera and Keystone—that'd be our home port—without at least one good, hard bump in the road along the way. Pirates, marauders, authorities, and rough weather. You ain't *seen* a storm until you been up in the teeth of the thing. You think you can handle that?"

"Again, if that's what it takes."

"Good. Now, since you're new to this sort of thing, let me explain a few things. This here ship is what we'd call a zephyr. Meant for a crew of sixteen. Of course, it's also meant for short trips along the coast of the mainland. To make room for the extra fuel and to make space for the cargo we need to make it worth the trip to places like Caldera, we've been running it with a crew of six. Everybody doubles up on tasks and then some. Long and short of it, we don't have room for tourists. You'll need to pitch in. For most Calderans I've met, that'd be a problem, what with their delicate clothes and fancy colognes and their dainty hands that ain't never seen the handle of a shovel. You look like the sort who knows how to put in a decent day's work, though. You know how to use them wrenches?"

"Some artists use a brush; I use a wrench."

"That's fine. You'll be working with Gunner, then. He's our armory officer. Let him know you're under him, and that I'll be taking the helm back shortly. Make sure you get introduced around, too. Maybe in your neck of the woods you can jump unescorted onto a ship of strangers and not have to worry your pretty head about it, but not where I come from. Best to show a friendly face in a hurry. It'll make it easier for us to do good by you and harder for us to do bad. Things are rough out here, and you're going to need someone to watch your back if you don't want to wake up with any knives sticking out of it. That means having some friends. You can start with me." He stood and held out his hand. "Cap'n McCulloch West. The crew calls me Cap'n Mack."

She stood and returned the favor. "Amanita Graus. My friends call me Nita."

"You look tired, Ms. Graus."

"It's been a long night, Captain. I work the night shift."

"See Lil or Coop about stringing up a bunk someplace, but see Gunner first. You'll find him at the wheel, back up on deck. He's the fella without the full complement of fingers." He picked up the coil box and handed it to her. "You'll want to keep this and the rest of the payment well hid. I vouch for my crew, but even so, you don't leave a steak out around a hungry hound dog."

"Um… where should I hide it, Captain?" she asked, stowing it in her belt again.

He puffed on his cigar. "That's another thing you should have thought of before you came aboard. As of now, you are the lowest-ranking member of my crew. You'll follow any orders they give that don't conflict with mine, and you'll have all the privileges they have, which is a mighty short list. Roundabout suppertime we'll all meet up in the galley, and we'll discuss the particulars of our little agreement, as well as how and when things are likely to happen. Until then, get good and acquainted with the *Wind Breaker* and her crew."

Chapter 4

Nita stepped out of the captain's quarters. She felt dizzy, and there was more to it than simply the pitching and swaying of the ship. Now that the impulse and certainty that had driven her to embark on this insane mission had begun to wear off and the captain's words had begun to sink in, doubt reared its ugly head. This ship and its crew couldn't be less like the world she was accustomed to, and while she certainly had been seeking something new, this was a good deal more than she'd had in mind. Nothing in her life had prepared her for this, so she defaulted to what she always did when things seemed out of control: calm down, focus on one thing at a time, and look for someone who knows what's going on. If she was to assist this Gunner fellow, then for now she would simply find him. Easy enough.

She pushed open the doorway to the deck and climbed the stairs. A chilly rush of air slapped her in the face, stinging her eyes enough to compel her to pull her goggles into place. When she could see again, she immediately noticed something very wrong.

The ocean was missing.

Minutes ago they had been just a few dozen feet from the churning blue waves below. Now there was nothing but the gray haze of morning above, below, and all around. The sun was only just beginning to rise in earnest behind them, providing a single point of reference in the form of a fuzzy red blob of light. It was profoundly disorienting, elevating her dizziness into stomach-turning vertigo.

Nita held tight to the nearest railing and tried to push the feeling aside. She scanned the deck for the others. Coop was nowhere to be seen, but Lil was tidying the coiled up moor line. When she noticed Nita, Lil walked confidently across the swaying deck. She wasn't wearing goggles, making do with squinting to cope with the rushing wind, and had donned a short jacket. It was clear why she kept her hair as short as she did. An inch longer and the wind would be whipping it against her face despite the bow.

"That was a quick visit. Everything go okay with Cap'n?" Lil asked. She leaned a bit closer and looked Nita in the face, then lit up with impish delight. "Oh ho! Looks like this is going to be a blessed voyage, because Nita here is fixing to make an offering!"

“What? I don’t…” Nita struggled to say, but her stomach put a quick end to the conversation by making a short but intense attempt to put her mouth to a more colorful use.

“Come on, darlin’. This way, quick.” Lil took Nita’s hand and led her toward the edge of the ship. “You’ll feel better in a minute.”

Nita didn’t have the will to object, simply stumbling along with Lil in a daze until she reached the waist-high railing at the edge of the deck. She held tight to it, closed her eyes, and took a deep breath.

“It’s not lookin’ good for this one,” Lil said to a crewmate, shaking her head.

“I feel… I feel a bit better. I just needed a moment,” Nita said.

“You sure? You’re still lookin’ a tad green round the gills,” Lil said.

Nita intended to assure her new crewmate that she was perfectly fine, but she made the unfortunate mistake of opening her eyes before she did so. Her head hung slightly over the railing, which gave her an unobstructed view off the side of the ship. Below them, a break in the fog provided the briefest glimpse of the sea below, but it was enough to make it clear that they weren’t *dozens* of feet from the water anymore, they were *hundreds*. It was the final straw.

“*There* it is! Oh Spirit of the Journey, please accept our humble offering of this greenhorn’s lunch in exchange for your good graces,” Lil said with her head lowered in mock prayer.

“I’m sorry,” Nita said, when she’d recovered enough to do so. “This is so embarrassing. I’ve been on a ship a hundred times, and I’ve never been sick.”

“Airships are a whole different beast. Happens to everyone on the first trip,” Lil said. “At least you were outside when it happened. You might want to carry a bucket around though, until you get your air legs. Were you after anything up here, or did you just want to feed the ducks?”

“I was supposed to find Gunner,” she said, pushing up her goggles to rub her eyes. What she wanted most was to find a corner to crawl into until she could get her head straight, but nothing was ever solved by being meek. Best to get to work as soon as possible. She pulled a small bottle of water from one of the pouches on her belt, rinsed her mouth out, and slid the goggles back into place.

“Atta girl! That’s him up there.”

Nita looked toward the prow and saw the man she’d briefly glimpsed during her first visit to the deck. He was working the controls. That was a mercy, at least. It meant he was facing away from her and hadn’t witnessed her little bout with airsickness. She straightened up and took a few plodding steps up the stairs, trying to judge the roll of the ship and move only when doing so wasn’t likely to tip her over the side.

“Hello. You’re Gunner?”

"That would be me," said the man at the controls in a far more crisp and unaccented voice than the others.

He was a few years older than the other crewmembers. If Nita were to hazard a guess, she would place him within a few years of his thirtieth birthday, though on which side wasn't clear. He was an inch or two taller than her, with black hair, a face full of stubble, and a pair of smoky and charred goggles keeping the wind at bay. His hands moved with a bit less confidence across the controls in comparison to his captain, a fact that may have been due in part to his hands. His right hand was missing the middle and ring fingers, and his left was missing the pinky. The injuries must not have been recent, because the brown leather gloves he wore had the corresponding fingers cut away and sewn up. He was of average build, dressed in much the same way as the rest of the crew save for a dedicated gun belt beneath his coat in addition to at least three holsters strapped across his chest and legs.

"I'm Amanita Graus. The captain said I should assist you."

"Are you? With what exactly?" he asked, tapping a gauge before muttering to himself, "Lousy thing's busted again."

"With whatever you need me to do, I suppose," Nita said. "He wasn't very explicit. He told me I would be working with you, and that he would be back to take the wheel soon."

"Well, that's good to hear. This bucket handles like a plow," he said. He pulled hard at one of the levers, conjuring a worrisome grind from one of the fans overhead. "I swear, I don't know how he gets it to do his bidding."

"I do it by treating her like a lady, Gunner," the captain said. He was stepping up from below decks, the freshly lit cigar clenched firmly in his teeth and streaming ash in the stiff breeze. "That means you need to treat her with care and finesse. Keep that in mind when you're showing Ms. Graus the ropes. And make sure she meets the whole crew."

"Aye, Captain," Gunner said, with a crisp salute. He stepped aside and turned to Nita. "Now, you're to be my assistant, are you?"

"I suppose."

"Well then, per the captain's orders, I'll give you the bare-bones rundown. No sense doing more than that right now. You're a Calderan I see. Am I correct in assuming you've never served on an airship before?"

"This is the first such ship I've ever set foot on."

"That's just lovely. Very well, we start at the beginning then." He released a frustrated huff. "This big sack over our heads is called the envelope. When we're firing on enemies, we aim for theirs and try to keep them from hitting ours. There are a few different sections in there, so we can stand a few holes without falling out of the sky, but not many. We stay up by keeping it filled with a concoction called phlogiston, which has got a great deal more lift than it has any right to. We go up and down by pumping phlogiston in and out of holding tanks with pumps there, and there." He indicated two deceivingly small mechanisms attached to the bottom side of the sack above them. "We're standing on the gondola, specifically the helm deck. Down those stairs is the primary deck, and there are three lower decks. We'll tour them shortly. The front of the ship is the fore end and we call it the bow; the back is the aft end and we call it the stern. Left is port, right is starboard. The deck numbers increase as you go down, with the primary deck as deck one. There, that's enough to get around, anyway. Am I going too fast for you?"

"I'm following so far."

"Good. If there's one thing we don't have use for, it's a slow learner. Now, introductions. My name is Guy von Cleef. The crew calls me Gunner for obvious reasons, and you may as well do so. You've met the captain already. Have you met Lil?"

"Yes."

"And Coop?"

"Yes."

"And Butch?"

"I haven't met him."

"Her, actually. Come along."

He walked briskly toward the stern of the ship, setting a pace that Nita found difficult to match without stumbling like a drunkard. All along the way he pointed his fingers and dictated terminology. Familiar mechanisms like pneumatic manifolds and pressure lines joined new terms like bottlescrews and ballast pumps. Nita tucked the information away, keeping track of a growing list of questions while focusing as best she could on walking without falling down and keeping what was left of her last meal where it should be. They walked nearly the length of the primary deck until they reached a hatch with a narrow ladder leading to the lower decks.

On what he indicated was deck two, they found the nearest thing to an open space she'd seen so far. It was a room with four picnic-style benches bolted to the floor. Each could, if pressed, seat three people on a side, and one had a cushion and white linen covering applied to the top, both of which had faded stains the color of rust. At the far end of the room was a half wall revealing a small kitchen stuffed to capacity. Its walls were hung with well-secured cutlery, their blades gleaming in the glow of the cooking fire. The air was muggy with steam and heavy with spice. A woman stood hunched over the far counter, but the steam and low light made it difficult to see any detail.

Gunner slipped the goggles from his face. "This is our galley and sickbay. Butch! I've got the latest newcomer. Mack wants her introduced around, as usual."

The immediate result was a torrent of foreign words spewed forth with an agitation and bitterness that transcended language. Butch turned around, clattering spoons and slamming lids on pots, and marched through the gate in the half wall without so much as a breath interrupting her incomprehensible tirade. She was sixty years old at least, and her voice was a coarse shriek that sounded at least twenty years older than that. She was heavy, with bulldog jowls and deep lines on her face, and dressed entirely in white, from the kerchief that held back her white hair to the simple white shoes on her feet. Covering her white dress was a lightly stained smock.

Her angry rant came to an end as suddenly as it started, and she stared expectantly at Nita.

"I'm sorry, I didn't understand," Nita said.

"She wants to know your name. She also said a great deal of very colorful words about people who interrupt her cooking, but it wasn't really relevant to the subject at hand, and I'd rather get through this quickly," Gunner explained.

"I'm Amanita Graus."

"Glinda West," said the woman, followed by what Nita hoped was a foreign pleasantry of some kind.

"West? Are you the captain's sister?"

"Ex-wife," Gunner said.

"Oh. Pleased to meet you," Nita said, holding out her hand.

Again there was a brief rant with a greater than usual amount of hand waving.

"Butch has a strict clean-hand policy. No handshakes."

"Oh, very well," she said, offering a curtsy, or as near as she could offer without wearing an actual dress.

Butch seemed mollified and offered a short statement that was, for once, not screeched like a harpy.

"She's sorry to hear about your mother, and she hopes we can finally pry some real medicine out of the fug folk."

"Thank you for your kindness."

The woman nodded once and turned, walking back to the kitchen.

"Butch is our cook and medic, so if you stick around it'll, pay to be on her good side," Gunner said quietly as they left. "If you happen to figure out how to manage that, be sure to let the rest of us know."

"What's that language she's speaking? I don't recognize it."

"To tell you the truth, I don't know. You'll learn to understand her though, if you make it as a crewmember."

"Why do you call her Butch?"

"That's not really relevant to the orders I was given." He progressed down the hall, pointing out rooms as he went. "These are strong rooms, filled with the goods we sell and the goods we get in return," he said. "They are locked tight, and only the captain has the key."

"If this is where you store the goods, what do you keep in the cargo hold?"

"If we could afford an airship with a proper cargo hold, we'd scarcely need to risk our necks with a monthly trip to Caldera. *Wind Breaker* was built as a coastal patrol ship. We converted the additional crew quarters for provisions, goods, and fuel. We also managed to scrape together some better turbines, a bigger boiler… I suppose it is easier just to list the things we *didn't* modify. That would be… well, I suppose the primary deck and the armaments. This ship has a pretty good set of teeth. Two sets of fore cannons, one set of aft. We try not to fire the aft cannon. It tends to knock the galley around a bit." He indicated the final pair of rooms on the floor. "These rooms are the only remaining crew quarters. This one belongs to the Cooper siblings. This one is shared by myself and Butch. There is no spare, so you'll either be stringing up a hammock with the Coopers or staking out a spot elsewhere."

"Yours and Butch's room is off limits?"

"No more so than the Coopers' or anywhere else on this ship. To be frank, I don't want to waste my time moving my stuff to make room for a greenhorn who's just as likely to not last more than a day with us."

"Don't write me off so soon. I'm sure I can be an asset."

"Yeah, so did the rest of them."

"And that happened to them?"

"They didn't cut it. It's that simple. So you'll excuse me if I don't feel inclined to move my collection for someone who won't be with us for very long."

"Collection of what?"

He pushed open the curtain. One half of the room was tidy and included a neat hammock hanging with a sheet and comforter arranged on top in what must have been the nearest equivalent to a made bed as one was likely to find on a ship. The other side was like an armory, or perhaps a museum of the history of warfare. It had almost as much gleaming cutlery secured to the walls as the kitchen. Swords, daggers, and knives were joined by flintlock pistols, revolvers, rifles, shotguns, a multibarreled contraption with a crank on the side, and some sort of tube that she would have guessed was a musical instrument if not for the company it kept.

"Assorted firearms, bladed weapons, and bludgeons. Some precataclysm antiques, some original creations, all fully restored and functional."

Nita watched as a particularly strong shift of the ship jostled the wall-mounted portion of the collection, much of which was directly over his hammock.

"Aren't you afraid something might fall on you?"

"It only happened once, and the scar is barely noticeable. I still contend that Coop was playing with my cutlass and didn't return it to its mounting properly." He cut himself off, shaking his head and chastising himself under his breath. "Never mind. Doesn't matter. Waste of time. Onward to deck three, which is more or less our utility deck."

He led the way to another ladder and brought Nita to deck three. By virtue of the shape of the ship, this deck was somewhat shorter than the one above. It was primarily an I-shaped hallway running past six rooms, three on each side, and two larger rooms at the far ends.

"The fore and aft rooms hide the workings of the cannons. The ammo hoists and such. If you're to be my assistant, you'll spend much time in there, so no need to open those doors for now."

"If you don't mind, I would love to get a look at them. I've always been fascinated with machinery."

"I was asked to show you around and introduce you. I prefer to get my orders out of the way as quickly as possible, so I can return to more worthwhile diversions, if *you* don't mind."

Nita eyed Gunner. Lil and Coop were kind enough at first blush to make her wonder if she'd been misinformed about the overall attitude of outsiders. Gunner seemed determined to even the balance.

"The primary powder magazine is up this way, just ahead. The secondary powder magazine is back that way. Over here is the boiler room, water tanks, and immediate fuel supply. No need to take you downstairs. Just the gig hoist and the fuel, water, and gas storage. Oh, actually, you'll find the head there as well, when nature calls. With that, I believe that fulfills my orders. All introductions, and a quick tour."

"One moment... Lil, Coop, Captain Mack, Butch, and you. That's five crewmembers. Where is the sixth?"

"Sixth? We don't... oh, Captain Mack was counting our inspector. Since he wasn't in the galley or with the captain, he'll probably be in the boiler room."

He took a few strides down the hallway and pulled open one of the few solidly shut doors in the ship to reveal baking heat and a sooty atmosphere that was almost like a taste of home for Nita. She found herself strangely excited to finally see something the she was confident she would know inside and out. After all, a boiler is a simple mechanism. Surely one design could only differ so much from another. This one would be smaller than the boilers back at the steamworks, but all of the components would be the same. When she got a glimpse of the thing, she realized how very mistaken she was. The scale was the least of the changes. This contraption bore little or no resemblance to any such device she'd seen, even the wood-fired ones she'd seen in ships. It almost looked inside out. There was a firebox, steam and water pipes, and a chimney. All parts she'd expected to see, but joining them was a bird's nest of tubes both large and small, twisting over themselves in a brass, copper, and cast-iron nightmare.

"*This* is your *boiler*?" she asked, waving off a particularly strong whiff of the odd-smelling fumes that hissed from the firebox door.

"Of course. Technically this is also my responsibility, but it isn't as though there's much to do."

"Not much to do?"

"Just shovel some fuel into it now and then, refill the water tanks, blow out the brine, and swap out the bits that wear out. And we'd better hope there's not much of that, because we're down to just the one spare."

"I've been working as a free-wrench in the largest steamworks in Caldera for years, and I haven't come close to mastering the different trades. Boilers need constant upkeep and inspection. I assumed that's why your inspector would be in here. Where is he, anyway?"

"Oh, he's probably up in the dark corner over there. He likes it warm," Gunner said. He leaned down and tapped the floor. "Come on out, Wink. There's another one."

Nita raised an eyebrow, then took a step back when *something* stirred in the darkness. When it revealed itself, slinking into the glow of the fire, getting a good look did little to clarify what it was. It was a creature with wiry, ghostly gray fur. At a glance she might have thought it was a cat based on the size, but the illusion didn't last long. The ears and nose were batlike, and as it moved toward them it demonstrated the awkwardness of something more at home in the trees than on land. A few short hops brought it to their feet, where it flicked its long, fuzzy tail and looked at them with a perfectly round red eye. The other eye was hidden beneath a cloth sash tied about the creature's head. It turned to Nita and crouched down, drumming its spidery fingers without taking its eye off her. Nita took a step back, not sure what to make of it, but quite sure she didn't want to be touched by it.

"What *is* that?" Nita asked.

"That's our ship's inspector, Wink. The fug folk require at least one of them to accompany every ship. They tap along the planks looking for wood grubs, which we can pick up from time to time when we make landfall. They're also trained to identify and mark planks that are succumbing to rot. Mack says this ship would have fallen apart years ago without Wink here, so he usually considers him a crewmember. Rather silly sentiment, if you ask me, but captains all have their quirks."

"But what manner of creature is it?"

"Some sort of jungle creature. They come from an island on the far side of Rim. At least that's where they *came* from. Now they mostly come from the fug, and who knows how the fug folk get them. Enough of that, though. The captain's order is followed to the letter. I've got to rest up for my watch.

Get yourself sorted out. I suppose I'll figure out what to do with you in a few hours."

Gunner ushered Nita out of the boiler room. Wink lingered in the still-open door. She stared down at the creature, and it stared right back. Its face had a stern, almost distrustful look as it met her gaze. With a final jittery tap of its thin fingers, it slunk into the shadows within and shut the door. It was astounding how ominous such a small creature could be.

Chapter 5

Nita fidgeted uneasily in her freshly installed hammock. Space was the most precious thing on the ship, and as such there were few places where she might find a corner to call her own. She'd settled on hanging her hammock in the room they called the gig room, the room through which she'd entered the ship. Despite the piled boxes of their less valuable merchandise, it had the most free space. Within minutes of setting down to rest she regretted her decision. Though the dinghy was winched tightly to the bottom of the ship and the other hatch was shut, they didn't create an airtight seal. As such, she was treated to the whistling of wind all night long. The constant motion of the ship had a habit of swinging her hammock so violently that at times she was worried she would fall out. They'd provided a blanket, and a second one to roll up as a pillow, but for someone so used to tropical climes it was still a bit chilly even in her heavy work gear. By far the worst part of those first few hours of rest, though, was the time it gave her to think.

There was no aspect of this journey that sat well with her. It was uncomfortable, but that much she could stand. The air had a strange smell to it, either from the fuel they burned in the boiler, the gas they filled the envelope with, or the particularly lax approach to hygiene shared by certain members of the crew. Rather than the shower she'd unwittingly come to rely upon to relieve the stresses of her day, the best this ship could offer was a bucket of clean water, a cake of soap, and a sea sponge, all tucked into a small room at the stern of the ship. The added presence of a washboard suggested that the room doubled as laundry facilities. In the opposite corner was the bathroom, or "head" as they called it, though even that seemed to be too extravagant a name for what turned out to be a bench mounted over a hole in the bottom of the ship. Using it was an unpleasantly breezy experience that made her feel sorry for any fishermen or sailors who might be below. It also served to remind her of the one fact she could never come to terms with; she was hundreds of feet in the air in a none-too-sturdy vessel.

Such thoughts had been churning in her head for three or four hours, making sleep all but impossible, when a tapping sound drew her attention. In the doorway was Wink, or rather *on* the doorway. He was crawling up with ease, tapping with his middle finger and cupping his ears toward the sound. Nita tried to put him out of her mind and get back to sleep, but something seemed odd. The tapping had slowed and stopped. She turned, but as soon as she moved, Wink started tapping again with renewed vigor. Twice more she looked away and twice more the tapping trailed off. She pulled the goggles from her bag, buffed the lenses a bit, and pretended to drift to sleep once more. When the tapping began to slow, she tipped them enough to see Wink in the reflection. He was staring at her.

At that point, it became clear she would get no more sleep today.

As it turned out, it was just as well. Not a minute after her brain finally gave up on being rested, the flared tube beside the door echoed with a bellow that she could just barely hear through the walls as well. It was Butch, shouting in whatever language she spoke. Though she couldn't understand the announcement, she assumed a trip to the galley was called for. She dislodged herself from the hammock and stumbled her way to the nearest ladder. At the top, she encountered Lil.

"There you are, Greenhorn. I was just coming down to fetch you. Supper's on the table. Or lunch. Or breakfast, I reckon. Just depends how long you been awake. You sleep okay?"

"Terrible."

"I did too, my first few days. Nowadays I can't hardly sleep without my hammock rocking in the breeze. Being a greenhorn is rough. I guess that's part of why most of you don't last more than a day."

"Why do you keep calling me that?"

"What, a greenhorn? Because that's what you are! A newbie, a tenderfoot. Wet behind the ears and all that," she explained. "Better get used to being called that. Round here, *everybody's* a greenhorn 'til the Cap'n decides otherwise. Life on a ship ain't all bad, though. Once you learn to look it in the eye without feeding the ducks, the view's a thing to see. Plus, on this ship you get to eat what Butch makes, and that stuff's fit to make your tongue kick a hole through your teeth to get at the spoon."

Nita grinned. There was something disarmingly charming about the way these people spoke. In Caldera, the desire to create ran so deep that people of distinction spoke with an almost literary formality. Thanks to the status of her parents, she dealt with such people every day. The clumsy but colorful manner of speech employed by people like Lil and Coop, whether purposefully or not, had an undeniable life and poetry to it. To ears trained from birth to seek out uniqueness and creativity in all of its forms, it was a joy. It was like finding a whole new set of colors to paint pictures with.

Lil led the way onto the galley, where all but the captain were already present and seated. At one table lounged Gunner. At another perched Coop. The third was empty.

"That there's the captain's table. You don't sit there unless you're invited. Anywhere else is up for grabs."

"Where *is* the captain?"

"He's getting the ship set to guide herself for a while. Once he's set a course, he can't leave her for more than a few minutes at a time before the wind sets us off in the wrong direction again, but a good look at the wind gauge and some careful figuring can usually get him time enough to come down and have a meal. Of course, that's assuming he hasn't got that feeling he gets when he decides he can't leave the deck, which is as often as not. He's a mite skittish about not having at least a lookout up there."

"Me bein' a mite skittish is what's kept this bucket in the sky instead of in the drink, let's not forget. And it's hazy out there. Low clouds. Let's make this quick so I can put someone out there on lookout," Captain Mack said, marching in through the doorway.

Nita took a seat at Lil and Coop's table. A shallow notch cut into the table formed just the right size to fit the bottom of a bowl, and another was sized for the bottom of a mug. When the captain was seated, Butch emerged from the kitchen with a pile of tin bowls, mugs, and spoons stacked precariously in one arm. She fitted them into the table in front of each of the crewmembers, never once so much as allowing the pile to teeter despite the motion of the ship. She then fetched a heavy pot and spooned out their dinner.

After Lil had bragged about it, Nita had to admit she was curious and a little excited to see what sort of exotic food these strange people ate, but what she got was a far cry from the irresistible feast the younger Cooper had described. It was a stew, or, at the very least, that was the closest word in her culinary lexicon that might describe it. What poured out of Butch's ladle was a wet mound of ingredients that had been boiled far beyond the point of recognition. The mixture probably included some vegetables, and *possibly* some meat, but each had given up and dissolved into a mush with the texture of mud and the color of paper pulp.

"I'm sorry but, um… what do you call this dish?"

"That's a bowl," Coop said.

"She means the food *in* the bowl, dopey. That there's slumgullion. Don't let the looks fool you. That's about as close to heaven as your tongue is gonna get."

Nita gave the bowl another doubtful look as her mug was filled with what smelled like ale. Never one to appear ungrateful, and with little recourse for anything better, she dipped her spoon into the runny mush and gave it a taste.

"It's… it's actually quite good!"

"You'd best get some of that shock and wonder out of your voice before Butch's feelings get hurt," Coop said.

"My apologies," she said, bowing her head. "It really is delicious."

"Like I said, one of the good bits of working on this here ship," Lil said.

"Let's just get down to business," the captain said. "As you all know, Ms. Graus here has a relative who is in a bad way. Needs some medicine that Glinda says the fuggers will have. She's offering the biggest payment we're ever likely to see in exchange for getting her some, so we're going to be spending a few extra days in port at Keystone while we try to get some out of those tightfisted beanpoles."

"Suits me. I got a pretty lady back that way who's probably staying up nights waiting for me to spend more'n a few hours in town."

"Sure you do…" Lil jabbed.

"If we're going to make it where we need to go, we're going to need to find a way for Ms. Graus here to pull her weight. So…"

"Do we *really* need to go through this *again*?" Gunner snapped suddenly.

"Gunner…" the captain said sternly.

"Let's just pitch her over the side now. The longer we wait, the harder it will be to do it when the time comes."

"What?!" Nita cried, jumping to her feet.

"Settle down, Nita," Lil said, putting a hand on Nita's arm.

"Settle *down*?! He just threatened to throw me overboard!"

Her hand clamped down harder, and the other revealed a cocked pistol. "Wasn't a suggestion, Nita."

Across the table, Coop pulled a pistol of his own, as did the captain. Gunner unholstered two things which might have been pistols as well, though they seemed to have more optics and barrels than could ever reasonably be called for.

"Have a seat, Nita. I'll explain what this is about. Gunner, on deck for lookout, and we'll discuss this little outburst later."

An angry sneer on his face, Gunner eased the hammers down on his weapons and stalked out the door. Nita looked to Lil and Coop. They still had their weapons steady, and most worrisome of all, their faces remained as chipper and friendly as ever. As there were few other options, she lowered herself to her seat.

"Are you going to kill me?" Nita asked.

"Not necessarily," Lil said. "All depends on how good of a job you do."

"Am I a prisoner?"

"Of course not. You're a greenhorn," Coop said.

"Ms. Graus, what you need to understand is this. You grew up in Caldera. I can't speak for your upbringing, save to say it had to be a darn sight better than ours. Things out here… well, they're rough. We run ourselves on a shoestring, and not just because it's all we can afford, because it's all we can *get.* A bad bit of weather puts us more than a day behind, and we start going hungry. A piece of equipment fails, and we can't be sure we'll make it at all. What we have on board is enough fuel and supplies to get five humans and Wink to the next port without much room to wiggle. And what we have right now is one human too many. I can get us through, all of us through, on what we've got, but only just. And *only* if everything goes right that can go right, and nothing at all goes wrong. That means if you show yourself to be a liability in even the smallest way, you aren't just a nuisance, you're a threat to our lives and our livelihoods. I can't allow that, not on my ship."

"How many times have you taken someone on board like this?"

"Oh, what is it now… seven? Including Nita here?" Coop said.

"No, no. It's nine, right? There was that couple who wanted to go from Westrim to Circa, and we got blown off course," Lil said.

"Right, right. Nine then."

"And how many have made it?"

"Well, there's still just the five of us on the crew," Lil said. "Plus Wink. So it's safe to say that none of them turned out to be worth their salt as airmen."

"But I think… well, I guess it was… nine take away…" Coop struggled with the math for a moment. "Cap'n, help me out here."

"The last two people are the only ones we had to take care of personally. One got himself killed, and the rest got back to shore, at the very least. Gunner had to do the deed for the ones that were more harm than good. He didn't take it well."

"But you *did* kill two people."

"We ain't killed nobody. Them folks just didn't turn out to be handy enough to keep themselves alive," Coop said.

"You people are monsters!"

"We're survivors. Sometimes being a monster is what it takes," Captain Mack said.

"Why didn't you *tell* me that if you decided I wasn't worth the risk you'd just kill me?"

"Well, because then you wouldn't have given us the money and come aboard," Lil said. "Even *I* know that."

"Ms. Graus. No one wants anything to happen to you, but the crew is my family. You'll do anything to help your mother, and I admire that, but I'll do anything to protect my crew just the same. Any way you see fit to feel about us is pretty well justified, ma'am, but here's the truth. If we were murderers, you'd already be dead. If we were thieves, you and your friends would be picked clean and cursing our names back down where we met you. We are all as good as this world will let us be. I mean to keep my side of the deal for you. I'll see those fuggers and I'll try to get you your medicine. But now you know the risk we're all taking to bring you aboard and the length we're willing to go to live to regret it." He holstered his weapon. "Now get some food in you, and we'll get back to discussing matters."

Lil released Nita's arm but kept her weapon handy. Coop did the same. Neither one of them had even once let their cheery expressions dim.

"Eat up. That stuff's not half as good when it's cold," Coop said.

Nita's heart raced, and her mind was flooded with conflicting demands to flee or fight, but she tried to wrestle the panic under control and reason with herself. She knew there would be dangers, and what they said was true. They could have easily killed her already if that was their plan. What could she do now? Wrestle the weapon away? Demand to be taken where she needed to go? She needed them now, but considering the full basis for trusting her hosts hinged upon the fact that they hadn't decided to kill her yet, the relationship wasn't likely to be a strong one. So she took her seat and shakily spooned up more of the stew.

"We're planning a straight shot to Keystone. The trip's just shy of fifty hours, if we keep this speed. Once there we'll unload our goods, resupply, and I'll see if I can get you a face-to-face chat with our supplier down in the fug."

"So we'll only be in the air for two days?" Nita said. "Surely *anyone* can avoid being a liability for just two days."

"Like I said, Ms. Graus. You're not going home for a month."

"But you could leave me in Keystone until it is time to take me home."

The captain gave a grim chuckle and took a sip of his ale. "You don't know Keystone. Leaving you there isn't much better than heaving you overboard. As I was saying. We ain't never got ourselves any medicine, not real stuff like that. Most folks have to go down there in the fug to get anything from their doctors, but with Ms. Graus, that might be different."

"Why's that, Cap'n?"

"She's Calderan. Two things fuggers like. Making money and finding new ways to make money. They're going to want to talk to her, to see if the time's finally come and the Calderans are ready to start opening trade with the fug folk like everyone else is. If anything'll get them to pry open the vault and let us get some of the good stuff, it's that. Hell, if we're lucky, we'll convince them to sell us enough to spread around a bit. Maybe get some worthwhile stock in the local hospitals, so we don't have to send so many people down there."

"That'd be nice. It costs an arm and a leg to get them folk to part with anything important," Nita mused.

"Let's not get our hopes too high. Anyways, if we get lucky and the fuggers offer to sell us your medicine, Ms. Graus, then naturally you'll have to agree to pay whatever they ask. I hope you've got enough in that bag to afford a pretty dear price on top of the box of trith and the jewelry you agreed to pay us to take you there."

"I've got plenty," she said.

"Glad to hear it. Then that's our chance to get what she wants. If the fuggers aren't so obliging, or the price is too high, then I'm afraid that's as far as we can take it. They aren't the sort to change their mind, and we haven't got the pull with them to chance getting on their bad side."

"What happens to me then?" Nita said.

"We keep you on the crew until our next trip to Caldera and send you on your way, less the money it took to feed you and such."

"Assuming I don't turn out to be too much of a burden along the way," Nita said.

"Naturally," Lil said.

"That all sound acceptable, Ms. Graus?"

She released a shaky breath. "I suppose I don't have much of a choice."

"In this world, most folk don't. Good that you're figuring that out so quick. It puts you two steps ahead. Saves you the time of hoping for better. Now enjoy your meal. Once you're through, we're going to have to see what it is you can do."

Nita nodded and tried to oblige, but finding out one's fellow diners wouldn't think twice about killing you has a strange way of putting a damper on one's appetite. Instead she nursed her meal and reminded herself that this was for her mother, and there was no other way.

Chapter 6

After dinner, Captain Mack sent for Gunner and had Lil take Nita to the boiler room for her first official task as a crewman: feeding the boiler. The young crewwoman led the way to the storage in the belly of the ship, chatting along the way.

"You still seem jumpy, Nita. Why's that?" Lil asked.

"Are you serious? I've had my life threatened by all of you. You pointed a gun at me!"

"Had to make sure you didn't do anything we all might regret is all. No harm meant, and no harm done."

"Is this really so common for you that you don't see how horrible it is to hang something over someone's head like that?"

"It's just the world, Nita. Just the way things are. Besides, you'll be fine as long as you lend a hand and don't cause any trouble. Ah, here we are."

She slid one of the heavy doors aside to reveal a room crowded with coal bins, as well as a stack of cloth-wrapped bricks of what looked like clay.

"Every hour we take four big buckets of coal up to the boiler room and dump them into the firebox, and one of these here bricks," Lil explained, pulling down the first of four buckets from their hooks on the wall and scooping it full.

"What is the brick?"

"It's... uh... well, to tell you the truth, it's got this big, fancy name, all sorts of chemicals and like, but we just call it burn-slow. You toss it in with coal and it—"

"Makes it burn slowly?" Nita ventured.

"Now you're gettin' it! These things cost a bundle. The fug folk make 'em, just like everything else these days, but we got to buy 'em anyways. With one of these in the firebox, we only need four buckets an hour. Without one, we'd need to shovel the stuff pretty much without rest. Couldn't hold *nearly* enough coal to get this ship to Caldera and back."

"Who *are* these fug folk who seem to have achieved such wonders?" Nita asked, scooping some coal into her own buckets.

"They're just a bunch of these twisty folk who live down in the fug. Real smart bunch, but not the friendliest folk. Real pale skin, skinny, tall, always hunched over. Probably smelly, too, livin' down in the fug and all."

"What is the fug?"

"You really don't know much, do you?" Lil said. "The fug's this deep purple stuff that's choked out most of the lowland in Rim. Nasty stuff. Can't breathe in it for more than a minute before you stop breathin' altogether. When Cap'n goes down to buy stuff, he wears this big mask, but even with that, you can't spend more than a day or two in the stuff before... well, before it'll make you wish you hadn't."

"It sounds horrible. Where did it come from?"

"Who knows? Before my time, but they say when it showed up, it took almost all the people from the lowlands with it. It ain't all bad. There's some fug in these lights here on the wall. You run some phlogiston through fug and it lights up good and bright. We call these phlo-lights. Even so, I hate the stuff. It's half the reason I'm out here in a ship. Good fresh air. Of course, the problem is Cap'n Mack takes such good care of his crew that I don't figure I'll ever get to move up higher than deckhand. Deckhand's just a fancy word for a person who does *everything*."

"Where I work, they call people like that a free-wrench. That was my job."

"So you and me are pretty much the same then. I feed the boiler when Gunner's on watch. I clean up the galley when Butch is sewing someone up. I..." Lil trailed off, her eyes turned aside as she listened. "Wailers."

"What?" Nita asked.

"Wailers! You'll hear them in a minute. We've got to get on deck!"

The pair dropped their buckets and rushed to the nearest ladder. Before they reached it, the ship changed direction suddenly and forcefully enough to throw even Lil against a wall. A steam whistle began to blare and the captain's voice bellowed out. "Wailers on port and starboard! All crew on deck!"

"What are wailers?" Nita asked, following Lil up the ladder.

"You're about to find out. Do you know how to use a rifle?"

"No!"

"Well, then you're on hook detail. They're going to shoot grapplers at us. Don't let them get on board! And keep your head down!"

They scrambled onto the deck just as the captain heaved the ship into another tight turn. A distant moan filled the air, drawing nearer every moment. It sounded like a low, continuous howl. Coop and Gunner were already on deck, each with firearms. Coop had a hunting rifle, but Gunner's weapon was truly massive, with two stout barrels and three lenses arrayed along their length.

"There!" Gunner called out. "Two on the port side, heading this way."

Nita pulled down her goggles and looked to where his weapon pointed. She spotted two shapes approaching faster than seemed possible. As they drew nearer, she could make out some details. They were airships, but vastly different from the *Wind Breaker*. They were tiny, the gondolas little more than metal tubes just large enough for two riders. The envelopes above each were thin, shaped like flattened pills. Behind the gondolas, single propellers spun fast enough to produce a terrifying wail, no doubt the source of their name.

Gunner fired his weapon with a thunderous blast. The force of it threw him from his feet, but his aim was true. A cloud of shot shredded the balloon above one attacker and sent him spiraling into the sea below. Coop tried to level his weapon at the second attacker, but a sequence of dull thuds sent him into a wild retreat. A row of five-inch nails traced their way forward.

"Behind the barrels, Coop. Behind the barrels!" Lil yelled, taking her own advice by sliding behind the relative safety of a trio of lashed down barrels on the deck. Nita dove after her.

"What are they? Pirates?" Nita cried.

"No, raiders," Lil said, drawing her revolver.

"What's the difference?"

"Pirates rob you and kill you, raiders kill you and rob you." She readied her weapon. "It's a *big* difference, trust me."

Another row of nails, fired from a vicious-looking contraption mounted on a third wailer attacking from the starboard side, peppered the deck.

"They're trying to kill *us,* not attack the ship. We just have to hold them off for a few minutes. Those little ships run out of steam real fast. *Down*!" Lil commanded.

A blur of hooked metal hurled through the space previously occupied by their heads, then tumbled across the deck. Lil planted a foot on Nita's back and heaved her out of the way in time for the grappling hook to reach the end of its rope and scythe back toward them. It bit into the barrels and tore them free, then splintered itself into the deck and held firm, yanking the ship lightly to one side.

"Get that hook out!" bellowed the captain as he maneuvered the ship into another sharp turn that caused one of the other attackers to score a glancing blow with his hook, rather than a direct one.

As the turn straightened out, a powerful thump sounded from below decks and the ship began to lose speed. The intensity of the moment gripped Nita, and suddenly the thinking part of her mind once again gave itself over to the acting part. There wasn't time for fear or reason, just the task at hand. Whatever that sound had been could wait. The hissing salvos of nails were a distant concern. The only thing that mattered right now was getting the grappling hook free. She slid to a stop where it had lodged itself into the deck, yanked one of the cheater bars from her belt, and wedged it beneath the rusted iron of the hook. The barbed thing was well planted, but she'd had more than her share of experience fighting with stubborn valves and levering sections of pipe into place. Three good heaves tore it free and sent it skipping up and away.

"There's still two of them! And keep your eyes open for the main ship, if these things are still buzzing this fast, the mother ship has *got* to be nearby," Gunner called out. He planted himself and unloaded the second barrel of his gun, but failed to catch either of their remaining attackers. There wasn't any time to reload it, but for Gunner that wasn't a problem. There was always another gun where that came from. He threw open his coat and pulled two pistols with barrels nearly as large as the shotgun.

The deck was in utter chaos. Whatever had slowed the ship had cost them most of their maneuverability, and without the speed and turns to keep the wailers constantly readjusting, their attacks became more frequent and more accurate. Dagger-sized nails cut through the air from both sides as the tiny crafts strafed the ship. Coop cried out as one of the spikes slashed across his arm.

"Brother!" Lil screamed, rushing heedlessly across the deck to her stricken sibling.

"Another hook, ready to fire!" Coop yelled as Lil helped him to the shelter of the stairs to the captain's quarters.

Nita turned to see a hook streak across the length of the deck and drop across the other side, pulling taut and chewing into the side of the boat. Even from her vantage point, Nita knew the hook was well out of reach. She wouldn't be able to dislodge it from the hook end of the rope. As the attacker continued on his strafing path, the rope swept across the deck, sliding along the top of the railing and catching her across the stomach before she could drop below it. She was dragged backward across the deck until the rope struck some of the rigging that held the gondola to the envelope, bringing it to a sudden stop and sending her sliding along the deck until she struck the next strut along.

The blow dazed her, but not enough to knock the sense of purpose from her head. She rushed back to the rope and fumbled for her knife. In the steamworks there wasn't much call for it, so she didn't keep the short blade in any of the more accessible places. As she fought for it, she noticed a regular jerk and vibration to the rope, and looked aside to see that the wailer ship was reeling itself in on a small winch. It gave Nita her closest look yet at the craft, revealing two pilots seated one in front of the other. The pilots were nothing like the crew of the *Wind Breaker*. Rather than dressing in what was very nearly a uniform, the two men were dressed in layered and mismatched clothes, heavy on buckles, leather, and improvised metal armor. The only things they both wore were padded leather helmets with built-in goggles, and maniacal bloodthirsty grins. The one in the rear seemed only to have the flight controls to worry about, but the foremost raider had a mounted grappler on a pivot, and a chain-fed spike gun in an immobile, forward-facing mount. As the grappler reeled in, the spike gun drew toward her.

She finally managed to pull her knife free and slice the rope just as the gunner fired his first shot. The brief burst of nails came close enough to tousle her braided hair behind her head, but with the rope cut, the sudden loss of tension caused the wailer to spin wild. While the pilot was still righting his craft, Gunner slid to the railing and unloaded the monstrous pistol, tearing through the vehicle's balloon and sending both riders plummeting.

"Mother ship sighted! Lil, Gunner, I want both forward cannons loaded! I'm taking these scoundrels out of my sky!" the captain ordered.

Lil and Gunner disappeared below decks, leaving the captain and Nita as the only able-bodied people on deck. A distant and familiar thump drew Nita's eyes upward to where the remaining attacker had fired its grappler. The hook tangled in the rigging, high over Nita's head and well out of reach, and immediately the gunner began to reel his craft in.

Nita thought quickly. She'd never be able to reach the hook, or even its line, and she didn't have a weapon. Her eyes darted about, first to the spinning prop of the attacker, then to the rope running across the deck from the previous grappling attempt. Acting more out of instinct than inspiration, she grabbed the rope and gathered up as much as she could as she worked her way across the deck. By the time she reached the opposite railing, the wailer was near enough for her to hear the two pilots barking orders to one another. She snatched up a dislodged chunk of wood the size of her forearm and quickly knotted it to the end of the rope, gave it a twirl, and heaved it toward the attackers that were now nearly overhead. Her aim was true, and the rope crossed the propeller, instantly tangling. The wailers' ship was yanked downward and twisted hard aside, dumping both pilots. One missed the ship and fell to the sea. The other struck the railing and held firm.

The ship was turning ponderously now, angling itself toward a larger airship that was partially obscured by a cloud in the distance. Nita had to throw herself to the deck to avoid the wild, riderless wailer ship that was still winding its prop more and more tightly and pulling it toward the deck as it did. When she got to her feet, she found that the surviving rider had wrestled his way onto the deck. Heavily armed, he held a saber in one hand and a revolver in the other. Still running more on instinct than common sense, Nita drew one of her cheater bars from her belt again and launched herself at the attacker. The surprise of the sudden attack managed to thump her attacker hard on the shoulder, but he recovered quickly and fired his weapon. Nita saw it coming and stepped aside, but a follow-up attack from his saber clashed against her raised bar with enough force to knock her from her already unsteady stance. He pointed his pistol, and, for a moment, Nita believed her end had come. Then came a call from the captain.

"Fire starboard cannons!"

Deafening thunder rang out, and the whole of the ship jerked aside as if struck. The force of it sent Nita's attacker stumbling back toward the railing and nearly threw him overboard, but he held firm. Out of the corner of her eye, Nita saw a burst of greenish gas as the wailers' main ship began to plummet. Her main attention remained on her own threat as the man recovered and raised his pistol once more. A second, quieter crack filled the air and the wailer jerked backward, dropping his weapon and cupping his hand to his chest. Another crack split the air, and the man, stricken, finally went over the side. Nita swept her eyes across the deck until she spotted Coop, smoke still drifting from the barrel of his rifle.

"Direct hit! Gunner, Lil, back on deck, now!"

Just like that, the battle was over, though not without its costs. The turbines above were sputtering and out of rhythm. The largely intact wailer craft lay splayed across most of the central stretch of deck, its envelope now dangling from a single line and leaking a stream of green vapor, its steam fans grinding. Before the fiery rush of battle could fully subside, Nita hurried to Coop to help him to his feet.

"That was quite a shot, Coop," Nita said. "Are you all right?"

"Been worse, ma'am," he said, handing over his rifle and investigating the gash on his arm. It was shallow but long, and bleeding copiously. "Dang it. This here's my favorite shirt. My favorite arm too."

Lil appeared from below decks and ran to her brother's side. "Big brother, move your fingers for me. Come on now."

"I'm fine, Lil. Nita and I held the deck just fine."

"You all right, Nita?" Lil asked, looking her new crewmate up and down.

"I think so. A little bruised, but nothing serious."

"You handled yourself pretty good, I'd say. I knew you wouldn't end up going over the side. And you didn't turn green even once while you were up here."

"Turn green? From what?" Nita asked. She looked about, then locked her eyes on the horizon. "Oh… oh dear…"

For the first time, the frenzy had died down enough for her brain to process her surroundings beyond a knee-jerk threat assessment. On the previous day the shifting of the deck and the realization of their altitude had been enough to make her sick amid a barely discernable haze. Now the sky was clear, and they were over a thousand feet high. The part of her mind trained to recognize beauty thrilled at the sight, a ring of endless sea in all directions, the sky a brighter blue than she'd ever seen it, and cottony clouds so near she felt she could touch them. Unfortunately the part of her mind charged with self-preservation, already stretched to the limit with the battle and shakily coming back to normal, wanted no part of this view or any other that wasn't firmly rooted on solid ground. It seemed determined to voice its displeasure in much the same way it had the day before.

"I think I'm going to—" she began, stumbling toward the railing.

"Belay that, Ms. Graus. There's still a job to do," Captain Mack barked.

Nita flinched, first wondering how he could possibly believe he might be able to order her digestive system to behave, then wondering why it had seemed to work.

"Cap'n, permission to take him down to Butch," Lil said.

"Do it," the captain said.

"When did *this* happen?" Gunner called from behind them, circling the remains of the wailer craft.

"I didn't have any weapons, and their grappler was out of reach. I had to improvise," Nita said.

Gunner nodded in appreciation. "I always did want to get a look at one of their fléchette guns!"

"Indulge your weapon lust later, Gunner. I want a complete list of all damage, inside and out. Take Ms. Graus with you. Teach her a thing or two. Lil, once you've seen to Coop's arm, I want you up here on lookout. It wouldn't be the first time we encountered two wailer ships at once. And I don't like the way the turbines sound. I'll have to stay at the wheel. It is going to be a fight keeping this ship on course. You have your orders. Move."

Chapter 7

Nita and Gunner walked slowly along the deck, cataloguing the damage. She did her best to avoid looking over the edge, as she wasn't sure how long her scolded stomach would remain obedient, and she was in no hurry to put it to the test again.

"Six more damaged planks. One will need to be replaced," he remarked. He turned to her. "You handled yourself rather well."

"Don't talk to me," she growled.

"Have I done something wrong?"

"You wanted to throw me over the side not two hours ago."

"Ah, that. I can see how that might strain our working relationship a tad."

"A tad, yes. These three barrels went over the side. What were they?"

"Rain water. Might be a problem, but not an immediate one. At any rate, I'm what you might call a pragmatist."

"No, you're what I might call an ass."

He looked up. "I don't like the way that bit of rigging is fastened. We'll need to get Lil up there to take a closer look. This is still your first time in the air, Nita,"

"You'll call me Ms. Graus until I say otherwise."

"Very well, *Ms. Graus*. The sun hasn't even set on your first day, and we've already been attacked. I don't know what sort of people you've encountered in your short life, but how many would you say could manage to function in conditions such as these?"

"Not many," she grudgingly admitted. "This pipe here is pierced."

"That's one of the captain's speaking tubes. Nonessential. Crewing an airship is a lifetime commitment, which isn't to say it is a very long one. Survival is rare and comes only at the cost of some very unpleasant decisions. We are alive because we've known when to cut our losses and trim the finger to save the hand." He held up his three-fingered right hand. "Literally in my case. And trust me when I say that losing a crewmate is no more pleasant than losing a finger. I'd rather cull the herd early than lose someone I've had time to know and work with."

"If telling me that advising my murder was motivated by your desire to avoid heartache in the long run is supposed to improve my opinion of you, it didn't work."

"So be it. I'd think twice about how you choose to direct your spite, though. Your life and livelihood still rely upon you doing a good job."

"I *always* take my job seriously, Gunner, even when my life *isn't* on the line. What's that up there?"

He looked where she was pointing. A very faint but unmistakable stream of green vapor sprayed out of the center of a patch on the envelope overhead.

"Bad news. Very bad news. Captain! One of the nails caught a patch. Not on a seam, slow leak. So long as it doesn't open any more, we probably won't have to lower our altitude for a few days."

"Patchable?" the captain called back.

"It's on the underside of the envelope, but tough to reach. It might be tricky unless we're at port."

"Anything else as bad or worse?"

"Not on this deck."

"Fine, get down to the boiler and find out what's wrong. We're barely limping. At this speed, we certainly aren't getting to Keystone before our supplies run out, and we're nowhere near any friendly ports."

"Aye, Captain."

Gunner led down to the boiler room, but before they were halfway there it was clear they wouldn't find any good news when they reached it. The hallway was dense with steam.

"This doesn't bode well," he said.

The door to the boiler room belched steam around its edges, and a bizarre rattle sounded, like an angry woodpecker was trapped on the other side. Gunner grasped the handle and gave it a pull, but the only result was a weak groan of wood.

"It's stuck. Give me a hand here."

She once again slid one of her cheater bars from her belt and wedged it into the door. Between the two of them, they managed to dislodge the door, releasing a blur of frenzied gray fur and angry chattering. Nita screeched as something scrambled up her leg, up her back, and onto her head.

"What in the world?! Get it off me!"

"Okay, Wink. Off there. Maybe this will teach you not to linger next to the boiler," he said. He plucked the creature from her head and set him down, then snapped three times and pointed. "On the deck, Inspector. Get to inspecting."

Wink peered up at the two of them, taking the time to give each of them their own dirty look, then hopped off down the hallway, stopping at the edge to stare at them and tap halfheartedly at the planks of the floor. Nita tried to shake off the bizarreness of what had just happened and pulled down her goggles. Gunner did likewise, and the pair made their way inside the boiler room.

Steam is dangerous stuff, and getting burned once is more than enough to teach someone the value of caution. It was clear by their deliberate motions and careful avoidance of all of the direct streams of steam that both Nita and Gunner had learned to respect it. This being the boiler room, the need for ventilation to feed the fire and remove the smoke meant that enough of the steam escaped to keep the chamber from being too hot to enter, but it was perilously close.

"This is bad," Gunner said. "This is very, very bad. The boiler is broken."

"Well, the room is still intact, and nothing seems scorched, so the primary workings are probably in good shape. All of that sharp maneuvering probably just put a bit of stress on the joints and ruptured a few."

"What difference does that make? The boiler is *broken*."

"Yes, so I'd imagine we should get to work fixing it."

"We don't fix boilers, Ms. Graus. We feed them, water them, blow out the brine, and replace valves. Only the fug folk fix boilers."

"I thought you were the ship's engineer."

"This ship doesn't have an *engineer*," he said incredulously. "*No* ship has an engineer. The fug folk don't leave the fug for the likes of us."

"Do you mean to tell me that the fug folk are the only ones who even *know* how to fix these boilers?"

"As I said, they are the *only* ones who fix the boilers, period."

"That's absurd! What do you do in situations like this?"

"We pray that situations like this don't happen, and if they do, we limp along and hope we get lucky enough to catch a tow back to the fug."

"Well, at least that explains why the captain would have made the armory officer the engineer. It struck me as rather questionable judgment to assign boiler maintenance to a man trained to make things explode. Let me see what I can do…"

"Don't do *anything*!" he said, pulling her back from the tangle of pipes.

"Why in the world not?"

"Do you know why no one knows how to fix these boilers? Because the fug folk don't *allow* anyone else to fix the boilers, or any of their equipment. If they so much as suspect you of doing work on their boilers, they'll refuse to service them ever again, and you risk losing trade rights with them entirely. That's the way things are done out here. This gadgetry is firmly in the fug folks' domain. We can patch holes in the gondola and rips in the envelope, but anything that goes clink when you tap on it is off limits."

"You make it sound like these people are your masters."

"Look. Life is just easier if we play by their rules, all right?"

Nita stepped out of the steamy room, already soaking wet, and pushed up her goggles. "What exactly *do* these fug folk allow you to do?"

"Well, they let us adjust the knobs and such, and they let us swap out these valves here." He reached inside and pulled their only spare valve from a crate just inside the door. "Everything else is done by them—or else."

Nita pursed her lips and thought. "Clearly some of the pipes are ruptured, we're wasting pressure. If we can shut off the pressure to the broken pipes, at the very least the intact pipes will have full pressure."

"And you can do that just by turning knobs?"

"Yes," she said flatly.

"Do it."

She shook her head and slid her goggles back on. "You people had the gall to suggest I would be a liability."

#

After forty uncomfortable minutes of working mostly by glove-addled touch in the steam-filled room, trial and error allowed Nita to locate the proper valves to shut off the flow to the broken pipes. The air in the boiler room cleared, and it ceased to feel like a sauna. By then the firebox, with its previous refueling having been rudely interrupted, was doing little more than smoldering. Gunner fetched the coal and slow-burn and dumped them inside. The pair of crewmembers watched as the gauges slowly rose on the active lines.

"There. That's about as good as you're going to get without doing any real repairs," Nita said.

"I'll go talk to the captain and see how this changes things. I think you've earned a few minutes of reprieve. In an hour, report to the primary deck."

Nita nodded and made her way wearily out the door.

"Good work today," he called after her. "Not just with the boiler, but with the attack. Good to see you're willing to get a little blood on your hands."

She nodded again, his words slowly sinking into her mind as she made her way to the bathing room, such as it was. Lil had given her a quick briefing about what passed for shipboard hygiene. It involved a bucket of nonpotable water, which, with the loss of the barrels on the deck, meant she'd be using seawater that was normally intended as ballast and feed water for the boiler. Then came the sponge and soap. She tried to put out of her mind the question of how old and frequently used each one might be. A few days baking under her leather and canvas work clothes had left her in a state that could only be improved by whatever hygienic measures were available. After she was as clean and dry as she was going to get, she changed into the only other outfit available to her, the dainty white dress she'd planned to wear home from work before she embarked on this unexpected adventure.

She was in the process of rinsing out her work clothes with the remainder of the bucket when Gunner's statement finally struck bottom.

"Blood on my hands…" she repeated.

That was silly. There wasn't any blood on her hands. Gunner had done the killing. And Coop. She hadn't… no. There was one, wasn't there? When she'd tangled up the final craft, one man had fallen. But that was self-defense. All of it was self-defense. She hadn't done anything to provoke those attackers, and she certainly couldn't have reasoned with them. Still… she *had* taken a life today. And it bothered her. Not that she'd done it, but that, until this moment, it hadn't occurred to her to feel anything but relief at having done it. She was supposed to be civilized. Civilized people didn't revel in the excitement of life-threatening situations. They didn't look back upon what had happened on that deck and admit, even grudgingly and only to themselves, that parts of it had been fun. Of course civilized people, as she'd been taught to define the phrase, didn't fly through the sky in wondrous machines. They didn't concoct new types of fuel that let them cross whole oceans. She shivered at the breeze in a dress that wasn't quite adequate for the chill and wind of high altitude and wondered if maybe the time had come to update her personal definition of civilization.

Chapter 8

Her work suit hadn't dried yet when the time came to meet with the captain, so she reluctantly made her way to the upper deck in her dress. For better or worse the ship wasn't moving as quickly as it might, so the wind wasn't quite as vicious as it had been on her previous visits. It still required her to hold her hands strategically and angle herself with care, lest an errant gust give her crewmates a show. She made her way toward the bow of the ship, taking a wide detour around the wailer craft that was still lying on the deck.

The captain stood at the wheel, and the entirety of the crew gathered around him. Coop seemed none the worse for wear. He hadn't even felt it necessary to change out of his torn and bloodied clothes. The slice through the sleeve of both his coat and shirt revealed a lightly stained bandage. Butch was muttering something unrecognizable, clucking over her patient it seemed, as he filled the breaks in her ranting with scolded assurances.

"I know, Butch. Don't lift nothing heavy with that arm for a few days. And drink lots. I'll do that too," Coop said, like a schoolboy enduring a long good-bye from a fretting mother. "Oh, look, Nita's here. We can get started."

"I'm sorry, am I late?"

The captain pulled a pocket watch from his vest pocket.

"Not quite late, Ms. Graus, but not early," he said, clicking it shut.

"Look at you, all dressed up in your finery," Lil said. "That's more what I'm used to from you Calderan folk."

"My only other clothes are still wet."

"You gotta let me try that on once. How come nobody ever brings a dress like that to trade?" Lil said.

"Because we don't never get no girls doing the trading," Coop said.

"I know that. You think I don't know that? It was one of them… what do you call it? Rectory-ical questions."

"What's church got to do with it?" Coop asked, scratching his head with his good hand.

"I think you meant rhetorical," Nita said.

"Is that the one you ask but you don't want no answer?" Lil asked.

"Yes."

"Right, I was askin' one of them."

"Now why would you want to ask a question but not want no answer?" Coop asked.

"To make me look smart, stupid."

"Let's get down to business!" the captain growled. "Ms. Graus's tinkering has got two of our turbines working at full strength, which is a damn sight better than they'd been doing, but still not good by any stretch. I'm bringing us down to the surface to take on water for the boiler. We'll drop a buoy to get an idea of our speed right now, but if I'm worth my salt, I figure we're not going more than twenty knots."

"How does that compare to our proper speed?" she asked.

"With a stiff tailwind, *Wind Breaker* can give us fifty knots. That's just about what I was figuring on us managing in order to hit Keystone in two days. There's better than two thousand miles between us and our intended port of call. At this speed, we're looking at five days. We were long overdue for a resupply even before we took on a new crewman. In a pinch the food will last, and we can always try for some fish if we come up short. With only two turbines running we can stretch the fuel. The problem is water. We lost a lot of fresh water in the attack. There's a bit of ale left, and we might be able to manage an extra day on the drippings we can get out of the steam lines, but we don't have the fuel to waste to boil up enough to be safe, and I don't like the idea of coming up more than a day short on water with so much chance for more trouble before we make landfall."

"You figure we've got to stop by the Lags?" Coop said.

"That's what I figure," the captain said with a nod.

"Would those be the Lagomoore Islands?" Nita asked.

"That they would. Though they've changed a bit since you Calderans closed your borders."

"I would imagine so. They weren't populated back then."

"They aren't populated now, either. At least, no more than a piece of meat is populated by maggots after a few days. A couple of enterprising traders took the place over, put up walls around all the springs, and otherwise found ways to wring a living out of the place. Resupplying there will cost us dearly, but it beats drying up, and it'll give us a chance to get a patch on that hole up there. All this presents a problem for you though, Ms. Graus."

"Why?"

"Getting down into the fug to talk to the fuggers isn't the sort of thing you do all willy-nilly. It has to be planned weeks in advance. Before I even leave on a Caldera run, I make sure to set one up. It is scheduled for four days from now. With three busted turbines, we ain't gonna make it, and this resupply trip is going to cost us another, or just shy of one."

"How long will it take to reschedule it?"

"Can't imagine it will be less than four weeks. Most likely you'll either be back in Caldera by then, or else you'll be with us for another month waiting for it."

"No," Nita said, anxiety in her voice, "that won't do. My mother—"

"I know it, ma'am, but it can't be helped."

"It *can* be helped. Just let me fix the pipes."

Captain Mack turned to Gunner.

"I told her, Captain. No repairs on the boiler."

"Let me just do temporary ones then. I'll remove them when we're closer to shore."

"Absolutely not. They'll know."

"I assure you I can do it in a way that won't show."

"Doesn't matter. They know everything that happens out here. They probably know we're here jawing about it," Coop said.

"That's silly. How could they?" Nita asked.

"Doesn't much matter how they know. They just know, and I'm not gambling that this is the time they aren't paying attention."

"This has gone from a bizarrely restrictive business arrangement to pure superstition."

"I don't mind a bit of superstition if it keeps my ship and its crew safe. And I'll thank you not to question any more of my orders," he grumbled, with the hint of a threat in his voice.

"Well… I…" Nita grasped at scraps of ideas. "At least let me look at the damage a bit more. If I get a feel for the way the system is laid out, maybe I can find a way to reroute some pressure to the remaining turbines."

The captain gave her a hard look, then turned to Gunner. "Gunner, show Ms. Graus everything she asks to see, and make it clear to her *exactly* what she can and can't do." He turned back to Nita again. "I'm giving you an awful lot of rope, Ms. Graus. Enough to hang yourself and the lot of us. So do us all a favor and don't go tying any nooses."

#

In minutes, Nita had changed back into her work suit. It may still have been wet, but she'd rather be damp and have all of her tools handy than dry and trying to get real work done in a dress. Now that she wasn't constantly avoiding streams of dangerous steam, tracing out the operation of the boiler was at least possible. One thing was certain from the first hard look at it; the thing was needlessly complex. There was undeniable genius in its design, from components that were more intricate than she'd ever seen before to linkages that were nothing short of inspired, but for every work of industrial art there were two unnecessary features. Pipes traced nonsensical routes, folding back on themselves and tucking themselves far out of the way. Manifolds of intimidating complexity split pipes only to join them together again. Scores of extraneous components were placed in just such a way that removing or breaking even one of them would severely impair the function of the whole system. In short, it was fragile by design, intended to scare away would-be engineers and remain *just* sturdy enough to get back to the fug to be serviced regularly by its creators. It was a testament to the brilliance of its designers that, despite the purposeless complexity, it managed to be easily twice as efficient as the boilers back home.

If she had a day, she knew she could remove and reuse enough pieces to get most of its functionality back. If she had a few weeks, she could probably throw away half the mechanism and end up with a simpler, sturdier boiler that they could easily maintain themselves.

"It wouldn't be difficult at all," she concluded after explaining as much.

"And in exchange for that we lose our trade privileges with the fug folk in perpetuity. I don't think you realize how much of their work and goods we rely upon," Gunner countered.

"They are taking advantage of you. Of *everyone*! They've been doing your work for you so long that you've forgotten how to do it yourselves."

"The advantage is theirs to take. And I'd keep my voice down if I were you. They are sure to hear you."

"How? From where? Are they lurking in the shadows, Gunner?" She picked up a manifold that had been entirely dislodged by the boiler damage. "Is this bit of pointless complexity a listening device? They've got you paranoid."

"Justifiably and stubbornly, so may we please move on?"

She sighed in frustration, throwing down the manifold and startling Wink, who had been staring at them with an indignant look since they chose to invade his domain. "You say you can replace valves, and we have one replacement. Where is it and which ones can it replace?"

He fished it out of the box and held it out to her, pointing with the other hand. "They'll let us replace any of these five valves."

"Well, those two are still working, and these two are on sections of ruptured pipe. This one was venting steam earlier, but if I followed it correctly, it only leads to the winches."

Gunner nodded. "Come to think of it, those are always breaking down. Best to replace it."

"What good would that do?"

"It would fix the winches."

"That wouldn't do me any good. I need the turbines working."

"You are a member of this crew now. It doesn't matter what is good for you, only what is good for the ship. You claim to be able to fix the whole boiler, let's see you do some work."

She nodded, more interested in getting back to her own task but not really able to argue with him. The procedure was the work of moments, something she'd done a thousand times back at the steamworks. When she was through, Gunner inspected it.

"Passable work," he said. "That's about all you can do in here then."

"According to the rules, anyway. These thick pipes here lead to the turbines, I think. They run up to the next floor. I'm going to try to trace them out again. Maybe there is something I missed."

"Suit yourself, but leave your tools so I can be sure you aren't doing anything you shouldn't. Perhaps you enjoy spending your time staring at pipes, but I've got a few hours of my own to look at that fléchette gun from the wailer."

"Oh?" she remarked, steadily dropping her tool sash, tool belt, and monkey-toe wrench to the floor. "I'm surprised the all-seeing fug folk will allow you to tinker with that?"

"It isn't part of the ship. They couldn't care less what we do with salvage."

Gunner stood outside the door, waiting patiently for her to join him in the hall.

"Why do I feel more like a prisoner with each passing moment?" she asked.

"Because you are new on the ship and the captain doesn't know if he can trust you."

He tried to shut the door to the boiler room, but Wink scooted out just before it shut tight. The little beast glared with its beady red eye, first at Gunner, then at Nita.

"You know, for all I've heard about this thing being the ship's inspector, I haven't seen it do very much inspection at all. All it seems to do is sleep in the boiler room or stare at me."

"He must be doing his rounds or we'd have shaken to pieces during those maneuvers, but as inspectors go, he's not the best I've seen. I wouldn't let the captain hear me say that, though. He loves that thing."

"I wonder why."

"I never cared enough to ask. See you at mealtime, and don't do anything foolish."

Nita nodded and set off toward the nearest ladder to find where the turbine feed pipes let out. Wink hopped along behind her, not taking his eye off her. It was the work of hours to trace out the maddening network of pipes again and again, trying to tease out an understanding of their layout. She stopped for meals twice, and once to sleep, but she was determined to find some way to keep to their schedule. Tracing the pipe runs from beginning to end more than three times revealed something new each time. Sometimes it was a new twist or turn that had escaped her notice on the previous pass, other times new valves presented themselves, or redundant connections turned up. Ginger taps to the pipes revealed that some were still getting steam, sending her once again to the start to find how it had gotten there and if it could be coaxed into running the turbines. A handful of adjusted switches and valves got the pressure as far as a leaky connection tucked deep in the space below some floorboards on the main deck that had been damaged during the attack. It must have been a troublesome connection even before taking a blow in the fight, because an ancient and moldy rag was tied around it, presumably in some fug folk approved attempt to get the leak under control. Now it was rushing with steam so viciously she could barely get near it.

"Ms. Graus. Sounds to me like some of those ailing turbines are showing signs of life," the captain called out.

"Yes, Captain. This maze of piping is finally revealing its secrets. If I can just find one or two more tubes between here and the turbines, or maybe knock loose a clog, I think I could get them moving again."

"Well, that's fine, ma'am, but until you do, shut the pressure back off. Unless those turbines are up to full speed they're just a waste of steam."

"Agreed." She reached down under the deck board and found the nearest valve, cutting the steam to the connection.

"We're pulling up on the Lags," he said. "I'll be taking Butch, Coop, and Gunner to help me fetch the supplies. You're here with Lil. We're going to let the boiler go cold while we're docked. I want the two of you to patch up the hole in the envelope, then scrape out the firebox and reservoir. Should get us another few knots."

"Aye, Captain."

"Ah! Ah ha!" Gunner crowed in triumph, the sound accompanied by a metallic grind as he pulled something free from the wailer craft. As Nita had been investigating the pipes, he'd been working on it with the same diligence and had managed to splay a sampling of the mechanical innards of the vehicle over much of the deck, piled in crates and baskets. "Finally got the gun free! And the grappler too!"

"Any use to us?" the captain asked.

"Both are steam powered. They'd have to be installed. You think we'll have the money to have it done?"

"Let's get there first. We can talk figures later. Stand ready, I'm bringing her down."

A grinding sound kicked up above them, the same one that always accompanied their descents, and the ship tipped forward a bit. Nita carefully worked her way to the railing, held tight, and looked to the horizon. After her embarrassing first reaction to the view off the deck, and twice more nearly repeating it, Nita decided the churning her stomach did every time she remembered how high she was would have to be overcome, sooner rather than later. The number of times her pipe investigations had taken her to the deck gave her ample opportunities to immerse herself in the frightening view. Sure enough, each time it lost a bit of its bite. The pitch and shift of the ship still turned her stomach, but at least now she barely felt a flutter when she looked to the sky and sea. She watched the green specks against the sea slowly grow larger, the tiny chain of forgotten islands she'd only seen on a map until today. The sun was setting, painting the sky a rich gold and sparkling against the churning waves. Now that the gastric repercussions of the view had been put to rest, the beauty of it struck her with its full force, and it was nearly enough to take her breath away.

Gunner walked up to the railing beside her. "Nice to see you aren't making any more offerings to the sea," he said, fiddling a bit with the liberated weapon under his arm.

"Look at it, Gunner. How can you help but be awed by it?"

"The Lags? They're one big cesspool of a place. What's to be awed about?"

"I mean the view. Do you know how many painters I know who would give their firstborn children to paint a landscape like that?"

"If you wanted to see the world, you shouldn't have closed your borders. Although I'll tell you that most of the world isn't half this pretty when you get up close. And something that's only pretty from a distance isn't really pretty at all, is it?"

"Beauty is beauty. It is present at any distance. You just need to learn how to see it."

#

As deeply as Nita believed that there was beauty to be found in anything, she had to grudgingly agree that some places did a better job of hiding it than others. The Lagomoore Islands, for instance, lost any trace of beauty once the ship was near enough for them to see the clusters of rusty, ramshackle buildings and smell the rancid and acrid smoke that rose from them. The perfect, little points of emerald visible from the sea revealed themselves to be cluttered with the remains of easily a dozen airships that had crashed or, judging from the looks of the people milling about on the shore, been shot down. The *Wind Breaker*'s lazy spiral downward took them on an aerial tour of the largest island, where three more airships docked. Each ship had a unique configuration, but they all shared a similar level of disrepair. The largest of them was clearly the patrol ship for the island, based upon the raw firepower it had on display. It had as many cannons as it had portholes and twice the turbines that the *Wind Breaker* had.

Whereas a sea ship needed little more than to drop an anchor near the shore to dock, things were somewhat more complex for an airship. The anchor was always an option, but seldom a desirable one. In this case their dock was a quartet of rickety wooden towers jutting up from the shore in a roughly square configuration. The captain maneuvered his ship as gently as he could, bringing it to a near stop as they approached the first tower, where a man waited. Gunner heaved a mooring line to the man, who scrambled to secure it. Once secured, Gunner threw a second line to a second tower. Once satisfied the towers would keep them in place and the mooring lines were properly taut, Captain Mack gathered his crew.

"We'll probably be onshore for the better part of two hours. Lil, Ms. Graus, your orders are simple. Patch the envelope, clean the boiler, and shoot any noncrewmember who tries to board the ship. If there's time left after that, finish disassembling that wailer ship. Leaving it intact might draw some of their brothers itching for justice, but the parts should be worth something. We'll be back with as much food, fuel, and water as we're willing to pay for in two hours. Be finished by then."

With that, he and the rest of his crew were on their way.

"Okay, you heard the cap'n," Lil said. "Follow me."

She walked to a supply chest on the deck, still sporting some nails from the attack. From inside she fetched a lidded bucket of what looked like pitch, then handed Nita a brush, a long hooked needle, a length of rope, and some thread.

"Come on. I'll show you the ropes," Lil said. She led the way to the base of the rigging below the leak. It was a narrow net leading from a set of tie-downs on the deck to some fasteners on the envelope above. She gave the rigging a tug. "These are them. I'll head up and get things ready. Give me the rope, then go cut a piece of the emptied-out envelope from that wailer you took care of. About... yay by about... yay," she said, giving a rough sizing with her hands.

Lil clutched one end of the rope in her teeth and scampered effortlessly up the rigging. Once she reached the top she threaded the rope it and lowered it back down.

"Now put the brush in the bucket and tie the rope to the handle, then come on up."

Nita tried to follow the directions. The first part was simple enough, but climbing the rigging turned out to be easier said than done. Nevertheless, she managed to reach the top with a bit of effort. Lil hauled the bucket up, tied off the rope, and pulled out the brush.

"The first step's easy. Just slather a bunch of this black stuff around and over the hole." She planted one foot on a knot in the rigging and swung out over the deck, reaching as far as she could and giving the fabric of the envelope a few good swipes. “Then you do the same to the cloth there. Not too much now. Then you slap it over the hole like that. Now the tedious bit. Gotta tie a sling so’s I can get a good angle on this.” She pulled up some of the slack end of the rope and tied a loop to the top of the rigging, then slipped her arms through the loop and stood against the rope, stretching the loop to its limit and positioning herself directly below the bulging patch. “Now you just sew it. Gotta do three rows.”

“You seem awfully comfortable dangling above the deck like that,” Nita said, a bit nervous just watching.

“Aw, you get used to it. You can get used to pretty near anything. Speakin’ of which, how are you liking life on the ship? Getting the swing of it?”

“I think I’ll be able to manage it for as long as I have to.”

“I can tell you, it’s great having another girl my age on board. Or just about, anyway. Being on the ship with a bunch of other men can wear on you. And there isn’t a looker among them. ’Cept maybe my brother, but regardless of what you heard, us folk from Westrim don’t date inside the family.”

“I actually haven’t heard much of anything about Westrim.”

“Well, it’s just as well. Pack of lies, the lot of it. Well, the bit about us being the best drinkers and the best fighters is the God’s honest, but the rest is malarkey and hogwash.”

“I’ll keep that in mind. How did you end up on a ship like this?”

“Not much of a story, really. Coop and I were from one of the flat-tops, you know, down in the south tip of…” She glanced to Nita, then smiled. “Oh, I forgot. You’re not from around there. Well, the folks who settled the west side of Rim just called it Westrim. Not a real imaginative lot, I guess. There’s some mountains down south with pretty flat tops, you know. They got a real name, I guess, but we just called them the flat-tops.

“Anyway, Coop and I raised goats there. I don’t know what sort of meat you get down in Caldera, but around here you either get goat, sheep, or if you’re real rich, you can get some beef from down on the plateaus. We were raising goats because they do good on the steep parts of the mountains. Problem was, we were pretty far down the slope, closer to the fug than we probably should’ve been. Along came a storm one day, kicked up the fug real good and just washed it right over our land. Killed the goats, darn near killed us, except we managed to get a couple of masks on, but that’ll only keep you safe for a few days before that stuff starts eatin’ at your skin.

"We couldn't see, we couldn't climb, and a big cloud of the fug was just sitting on us, but then down comes this ship. Cap'n Mack, back in his coast patrol days. He barely made it through the storm himself. Lost most of his men over the side. The only folk left were him, his wife, and Gunner. This was before Wink even. He dipped the *Wind Breaker* down in the fug and hauled us out. We said we owed him for that, and he said we could work it off, but really I think he was just finding a way to give us a place to stay, since our home was wrecked. He's a big softy. Don't let him fool you. Turned out both Coop and I were pretty good crewmates. So we stayed. Not a bad life, all things considered. And… uh oh, here comes Wink. He's looking agitated, something's up."

The creature shimmied up the rigging, then across Lil's legs. He hopped up and down madly and pointed with his horrifying strand of a middle finger toward the mooring line on the near side of the ship. The line was jerking at its mounting in an unnatural way.

"What is it?" Nita asked.

"Eh, it happens whenever we have to stop at the Lags. Move aside, but stay up here." She left the needle to dangle and drew her revolver.

Once she'd managed to shoo Wink off of her, Lil quickly descended the rigging and stepped up to the railing. A moment later a ragged-looking young boy no older than nine reached the top of the mooring line, a knife clamped in his teeth. He was greeted by the barrel of a revolver between his eyes.

"Hoo-wee! They sure are startin' 'em young these days, aren't they? I don't know what you're after, you little rodent, but unless it's an extra hole in the head"—she clicked back the hammer—"you ain't gonna find it on *this* ship. I think you should head back where you came from."

The would-be looter wisely chose to withdraw.

"Faster than that, shrimp," she said, squeezing off a shot over his head.

The child slid down the rope and climbed in a panic down the tower.

"Make sure you tell the other brats about the crazy lady on the *Wind Breaker*," she called after him. She brushed off her hands and holstered her weapon. "That'll keep 'em nervous for a while. You figure you can finish that patch up there? I want to get started on the boiler so the winch will be working to haul up the goods."

Nita looked uncertainly at the sling. "I suppose I can try…"

"You'll do great. Just remember, you need three rows of stitches. Pay attention to if Wink gets jumpy, and be ready to intimidate some punks if he does."

Before she could object, Nita's shipmate disappeared into the bowels of the ship, leaving her to once again muse over the remarkable way that the absurdity of this adventure was so effective at overshadowing the constant danger.

Chapter 9

After some initial difficulty, Nita got the knack of sewing while dangling from a hastily tied harness high over a deck that was itself high over the ground. Wink never seemed to show the same urgent agitation again, so she wasn't required to develop her punk-intimidation skills, a fact that left her both relieved and strangely disappointed.

She climbed back to the deck, Wink shadowing her as always, and made ready to join Lil in the boiler room. Her own experiences with cleaning boilers probably didn't have much in common with those on a ship. The steamworks boilers were large enough for a three-person team to climb into and had to be hoisted away from the heat of the volcano with building-sized winches. Even on the smaller scale of the ship, it was bound to be terribly unpleasant. She was heading for the nearest ladder below decks when something caught her eye. In one of the crates of wailer ship parts rested a pipe connection. She picked it up and turned it over in her hands.

"This... this might work."

Nita glanced around to ensure the deck was clear of any shipmates or other witnesses, then crept to the damaged floorboards and pulled them aside. She held the salvaged connector down to the broken one. It was a perfect match.

"Of course it matches," she remarked quietly. "The fug folk make these machines, too. It makes sense they'd reuse parts."

She turned the connector over. It even had a similar amount of wear. Her mind began racing in tight circles. She had been ordered not to make repairs, but this was such a small thing. It, along with her earlier judicious manipulation of the various valves and switches, would certainly get all five of the turbines spinning again. Lil was scraping away at the boiler, rattling the pipes across the entire ship. She'd never know this was even happening. No one would know.

The reasons to do it began to accumulate in her mind. She could restore the ship, get them back on schedule, and get a chance to negotiate for her mother's medicine. The only reasons not to do it were an order from her new captain and the vague and dubious threat of reprisal from unseen boogeymen. She hesitated, but only for a moment. All she needed were tools, which Gunner had required that she leave in the boiler room to prevent her from...

well, from doing precisely what she was planning to do. She crept up to the hatch to the lower decks.

"Lil! Do you need me to come down there? Or should I remain on deck to keep a lookout and get this wailer taken apart?"

"I'll tell you what," the deckhand called back. "It's kind of a tight squeeze. Not a two-person job. I reckon you should stay up there, keep an eye out and such, and slice up that ship some more like you said."

"Not a problem, but I'll need my tools."

"These are them on the floor in here, right? Well, come on down and get 'em! Just be quick about it, so's we don't leave the deck empty for too long."

Nita hurried down the ladder and into the boiler room. When Lil indicated there wasn't room for two people on the boiler-cleaning job, it was a drastic understatement. There wasn't even room for one. She had somehow wedged herself halfway into a hidden hatch near the top of the boiler and contorted into a configuration that human anatomy had never intended. She hung entirely upside down with both legs splayed outward at odd angles. Her upper body was out of sight, squeezed into a space that didn't appear to be large enough or even the right shape to conceal her. There was the constant sound of scraping, and bits of grit could be heard tinkling down to the bottom of the boiler.

"Are you okay in there?" Nita asked.

"It ain't my favorite job," she said, her voice distorted by the boiler's interior. "Lucky this only happens now and then. The *hard* part is getting out again. I might need your help for that bit."

"I'll keep my ears open," Nita said, snatching up her tool belt, tool sash, and—out of habit—her monkey-toe. "Heading back to the deck."

"I'll meet you up there when I'm done. It'll be before you know it."

Nita made her way quickly back to the primary deck. Repairing the connection took only a few minutes, but she nevertheless did it with great care. The whole enterprise would be pointless if the repair didn't work. She also kept a close eye on Wink all the while, lest another looter take advantage of her distraction and sneak aboard, but the ship's inspector seemed more interested in her own activity than the approach of an intruder. In no time she had the replacement part firmly in place and tied the moldy rag over it as it had been before. She then tossed the broken connector into the mound of discarded parts and got to work on disassembling the rest of the wailer craft.

#

Over the course of the next hour and a half, Nita tried to devote her mind entirely to the task of taking the wailer apart. On one hand, doing so gave her a fine education about how these fug folk built their machinery. Once she could get through the obscuring layer of needless complexity, the basic principles were actually quite simple, as all brilliant innovations seemed to be. Calderan technology was elegant at times, but that elegance focused primarily on using tried-and-true methods as efficiently as possible. The fug folk were just as willing to abandon the old ways as improve them, and in doing so they underscored faults in the traditional methods that she'd never noticed before. She found herself wishing she could observe this craft in motion again, so that she could see for herself just what the most mysterious innovations did.

On the other hand, immersing herself so completely in the task served to distract her from a rather insistent voice in her head. If it had been a voice of warning or fear, perhaps it might have made sense to her. After all, they *had* expressed a willingness, if not an outright eagerness, to kill her if she became a problem. In truth, fear accounted for barely a dash of the weight on her chest. She was quite certain neither the crew nor the fug folk would ever know what she'd done. What she felt most of all, regardless of what logic and reason had to say on the matter, was guilt. She was disobeying orders and violating a trust that she'd barely earned. No matter how pure or sound her reasons for such an act were, a part of her bristled against it. And so she dove headlong into her task rather than address those feelings.

She was just placing the last salvageable component into a nearly filled crate when Lil emerged from below decks. Her face and clothes were coated with gray dust from the inside of the boiler. The only portion of her face spared was the space around her eyes that had been protected by her goggles, giving her a reversed raccoon look.

"Phew! She was a stubborn one today!" Lil said. "I see you been busy. I'll bet we get a tidy little payment for that mess, huh?"

Nita held up one of the more complicated gadgets. "This is truly fascinating."

"Aw, it's all a big mishmash to me." She wiped her head. "I could use a bath something fierce, but it looks like I finished just in time. Cap'n and them will be coming back. I'll take over the watch up here. You go feed the boiler. Best to make sure the winch is good and warm before they get here. Wouldn't want 'em to have to haul the goods up the ladder."

Nita did as she was told, and the pressure was topping off when the gruff voice of the captain rang out.

"Lower the gig! We need to be loaded and off this trash heap two minutes ago!"

"You heard the man!" Lil called from above.

Nita rushed to the gig room and pulled the lever. Outside, the rest of the crew was quickening to a run by the time the boat reached the sandy ground beneath the *Wind Breaker*. Butch and the captain led a mule hitched to a heavily loaded wagon. Gunner and Coop had weapons drawn and eyes trained on the path behind them.

"You get in another disagreement, Cap'n?" Lil called from the deck.

"You stop flapping your jaw and get that ship unmoored! The fast way!" he ordered.

She groaned. "My share of this trip's profits better have a little extra in it this time!"

Nita ran to the porthole. It was coated with grime, but she could just make out the portside mooring line. Without warning, Lil dropped down from above, snagging the line and looping a leather strap across the top to slide recklessly down its length. One of the locals burst from the woods at the edge of the beach and started climbing the mooring tower, but Lil was already untying the line before he'd made it halfway up. She got the rope free, pushed it off the tower, and jumped to the ladder. She slid down and collided with the local at the ladder's midpoint, but a boot to the shoulder knocked him into the bushes and cleared the way for her to continue to the ground.

"Start the winch, Ms. Graus," cried the captain.

"But you aren't in the—"

"Now, Ms. Graus!"

She yanked the lever, and the slack in the chains began to reel in. The captain appeared and dragged out some boards from the floor of the boat to form a ramp. He led the mule right into the gig and off the other side, dragging the whole of the wagon over the low edge of the boat and straddling it. He unhooked the mule, scrambled aboard the wagon, and helped Butch to do the same. Lil sprinted by, heading for the other tower. The remaining two crew climbed aboard the wagon as winches began to groan and haul the precarious pile from the ground. Gunner aimed his overly complicated pistol.

"You're going to want to cover your ears. This one's got one hell of a report," Gunner said.

A crowd of pursuers descended on the beach. Gunner pulled the trigger. The sound was remarkable, more like a cannon than a revolver. It was enough to convince the mob to dive for cover.

"Is this the way supply stops usually go for you people?" Nita called down.

"On the Lags? More often than not!" Coop called back, taking aim with his own pistol and firing.

"Gunner, climb up and shut off the winches when we get close enough. Ms. Graus, get to the deck and haul in the mooring lines. Glinda and Coop, help me coax these dirty dealers to turn the other cheek."

Nita scrambled through the ship and up to the main deck. There were already return shots ringing out by the time she got there. Either the guns they were using were inferior, or else the envelope was tougher than it looked, because the bullets were doing little more than plinking off the turbines or bouncing off the fabric with a resonating *foomp*. She tried to ignore the insistent voice in her head asking where those bouncing bullets might end up and what was keeping the attackers from firing at her. There was no winch or reel to bring in the stout mooring lines, so she simply grabbed hold of the free line and threw it over her shoulder to drag it across the deck. Two more trips back and forth brought the free end aboard.

Captain Mack labored up onto the deck, his breath heavy and wheezing.

"Gunner, Coop, get ready to help her with the other line," he ordered.

"I can handle it," Nita said, crouching down to the rope and watching as Lil fought to release it from the tower.

"This one's gonna be a good bit heavier," Coop said. "How else do you figure Lil's getting on board?"

Nita's eyes widened and she looked to the tower again. The scrawny young crewwoman finally dislodged the rope and called out.

"Take 'er up!" she cried. She then glanced down to see a particularly brave local clambering up the ladder toward her. "And be quick about it. I got company down here!"

The captain took the helm and pulled hard on a lever, conjuring a grinding noise from above them and causing the ship to sharply ascend. Lil leapt from the tower and snagged the hanging line. She swung far under the rising ship.

"We pull when she swings away from the ship," Gunner instructed. "One, two, three, *heave*!"

Between the three of them, they were able to haul up half of the rope before she swung back. Another swing and another haul pulled Lil near enough to the deck for her to plant her feet on the hull and walk herself along it, with the help of a more constant pull, until Gunner reached down and dragged her up.

"Cap'n," she said breathlessly, "you wanna maybe give me the heads-up that you've got that sort of thing planned? I just got through cleaning the boiler and was powerful sore even before I had to go jumping off the ship and swinging around like a monkey."

"Did we just rob those people?" Nita asked.

"No, Ms. Graus. We negotiated a fair price and shook hands on it. Then they tried to say some nonsense about a docking fee. Far as I'm concerned, you break an agreement, you break the *whole* agreement. So we helped ourselves to the gear and goods and left what we figured they deserved."

"And what was that?"

There was the distant thump of an explosion. All eyes turned to the heavily armed airship that she'd figured for a patrol upon their arrival. Black smoke belched from the side, and the turbines on the starboard side had stopped, sending it into a slow spin.

"I left them a pyrotechnic demonstration," Gunner said. "Seemed like a fitting trade to me."

The captain looked over the controls, tapping a pressure gauge and adjusting a few levers. "On the off chance that one of those other ships is on their payroll, I'd say we'd best skedaddle," he said.

He slid a row of levers up, and the ship lurched forward, pitching down somewhat as the turbines roared to life... all five of them. At the unexpected acceleration and the full chorus of pumping steam, he turned angrily to Lil and Nita.

"I seem to be going full speed. Either of you care to explain how that happened?" He glared first at Nita, then at Lil. "Lil, did you leave the greenhorn alone in the boiler room at all?"

"No, sir, Cap'n. I was in there cleaning it up most of the time you were gone. She couldn't have done nothing, or I'd have known for sure. The only time she went in there by herself was to feed it with fuel a minute ago."

His glare turned to Nita again. "Did you do anything you shouldn't?"

"I was on deck, keeping watch and taking apart the wailer as ordered, Captain," Nita said. "As she says, I didn't have time enough with the boiler to do anything even if I tried."

"Probably cleaning the boiler out shook something loose and got them running again. You know how twisted up those boilers are. Poke around with one bit on one side of the ship and it causes all sorts of stuff to happen way on the other side."

The captain chewed his cigar and continued to hold the women in a measuring gaze. "Gunner, head down to the boiler room and have a look around. Let me know if it looks like she did anything." Gunner quickly obeyed. "You'd best hope he doesn't find anything. *Both* of you. But for now, make yourselves useful and load up the aft cannons. If one of those ships does come after us, I want to give it something to think about."

"Aye, aye," Lil said. "Come on. I'll show you how to do it."

Nita eagerly followed her crewmate below decks. With the *Wind Breaker* being as small as it was, the pair had reached the workings of the aft cannon before Nita felt they were comfortably out of earshot.

"Thanks for your support back there," Nita said.

"Who me?" Lil said. "Don't worry about it. You Calderans are smart folk. Help me with this door, would you?" She grabbed one side of a heavy wooden door on temperamental slides. Nita grabbed the other. "You wouldn't be dumb enough to tinker around in something after you were told not to. Now, this is the powder magazine. Gunner wraps these little packs of gunpowder in paper. Call's 'em charges. You're going to need at least one in each cannon. Cap'n likes a medium load, so that means two. And there's three cannons, so that… well, that's two each." Lil counted out two packs three times. Each was a cheese-wheel-shaped packet of brown paper about six inches in diameter. "Unless he says otherwise, we load with grapeshot. That's those little cloth bags down there. Grab one per cannon and follow me. Careful, they're heavy."

"Isn't it a little absurd though, not being allowed to repair your own ship?" Nita asked. She hefted one of the indicated cloth bags. It was almost as heavy as the monkey-toe strapped to her back and clacked when it moved, as though it was filled with individual chunks of metal.

"Rules are rules," she said with a shrug. She turned across the narrow hall and awkwardly kicked open a brace holding another set of sliding doors, then caught the handle with her heel to haul it open.

The doors opened to reveal the most concentrated mass of gears, chains, ropes, and pulleys that Nita had ever seen outside of the workings of the town clock back home. Three angled baskets dangled in the center of the space, and beside each hung a chain with a weighted pull, along with a separate loop of chain. The baskets were in three sections, one in front of the other, and were just the right shape to hold the bags and powder charges.

"Charges go in the middle, shot goes in the first basket, and when those are loaded up, you go back to the magazine and get a cap." She turned and fetched a metal disk. "These things blow up easy, so you put them last so you don't knock them around."

Nita loaded the baskets. "But prohibiting even simple repairs makes no sense."

"Maybe it's because I ain't the sharpest knife in the drawer, but most things don't make much sense to me. All I know is there's enough you *have* to do on a ship that it just isn't worth wasting the effort to start fooling with things you aren't told to do, or are told *not* to do. Now you just pull on this here chain until it goes up to the top and drops back down here empty. That means the cannon's loaded. You pull this chain, and that means the cannon's primed. Now when the captain wants to fire, he can do it right from the helm, or he can call out 'fire aft cannon,' depending on how busy he is, and we can pull that cord. Unless the speaking tube is busted, his voice will come out of the pipe right there. You can talk back too." She cleared her throat. "Cap'n! Lil at the aft cannon! Can you hear me?"

"Yes, Lil."

"You want us down here on reload detail, or should we report to the deck?"

"Report to the deck. Gunner just returned."

"Aye, Cap'n." She turned to Nita. "Easy as that. Don't look so nervous. This stuff hardly ever blows up by mistake."

Nita followed Lil back to the deck and willed her nerves into settling down. Her father had always joked that she and her sister would have made fine gamblers, because when they had a mind to, they could be as stone-faced as a statue. She dearly hoped he had been right, because the captain was already suspicious enough. Nita couldn't afford for him to see the same concern that Lil had spotted.

On deck, Coop, Gunner, and the captain were gathered around the helm.

"Ms. Graus, I had a word with Gunner," Captain Mack said. "You got anything to say?"

"Nothing, Captain," she said.

"And if I were to tell you that he found what you did?"

"Then I would have to ask to what he was referring."

He glared at her. She stared back with every ounce of stoicism she could muster. Finally he turned back to the controls.

"Nothing he shouldn't have found," he said. "Head down to the gig room and start unloading the wagon. Once that's through, tear it apart and patch up some of the holes in the deck. Coop will lend a hand."

Nita nodded and went on her way again. It took every last bit of will she had to avoid sighing in relief.

Chapter 10

With all five turbines back in operation, they were back on schedule, less the twenty hours they'd spent heading out to be resupplied. At that rate, if there were no more problems, they would hit Keystone just in time for their meeting with the fug folk. The journey turned out to be blissfully uneventful, though it was hardly restful. During the next two days Nita learned firsthand the amount of work it took to keep the *Wind Breaker* airborne. Once an hour the boiler was fed, and three times a day they dipped down to the ocean to take on enough water to keep the steam coming. Spare moments were spent patching up those things they could and creating a list of those things they couldn't.

Nita received a crash course in a dozen new skills, from carpentry to navigation. The only thing they never allowed her to do was take the controls. The captain reserved the right almost exclusively for himself, spending most of his waking hours keeping his ship on course. Gunner and Coop took the controls while he slept. Even during mealtimes he was more often at the controls than at the table. As Nita learned, this gave the other members of the crew a chance to speak freely about those things they would rather he not overhear.

"And that's the first time I ever heard the cap'n scream," Coop said, laughing and wiping a tear from his eye.

"You know, Brother, as many times as you tell that story, I still don't believe it. The cap'n would stare death in the eye. I don't reckon he'd be afraid of something as simple as a snake."

"I ain't sayin' he wouldn't stare death in the eye. I'm just sayin' that if death was a snake, he'd be screamin' like a little baby while he was doin' it," Coop said. He turned to Nita, "You got any questions about the cap'n, Nita? While he's not here is just about the only time you'll get 'em answered."

She took a sip of their recently acquired supply of something her fellow crewmates referred to as grog. The others seemed to love it, though Nita simply could not develop a taste for what appeared to be two randomly chosen types of alcohol mixed with copious amounts of questionable water.

"What I'm mostly curious about is how this crew came together. I know how Lil and Coop joined, but what about you, Gunner?"

"It isn't a terribly interesting tale, I'm afraid. I met the captain while the *Wind Breaker* was just another patrol ship. This was ten years ago, back when Westrim and Circa were just signing a peace treaty after all of those skirmishes. The governing council decided a few joint patrols needed to be put together to show we could work together. Little did I know the *vastly* divergent ideas of proper training held by the Circa Naval Academy and... does Westrim even *have* a training curriculum?"

"We do things the *proper* way," Coop said. "Conscription and apprentice... tion."

"And I can only marvel at the airmen it has produced. I was their armory officer, then as now, and the only fully college-trained member of the crew. Which means—"

"Which means he knows how to read books writ by folks who know how to do things, while the rest of us actually know how to do them," Lil said.

"Delude yourself as you will. To my great surprise, while the rest of the crew at the time was a damnable collection of misfits and imbeciles, the captain is remarkably skilled. Once that storm cost us most of our crew, he found himself this *new* pair of misfits and imbeciles, but at least they turned out to be quick learners. Not that they could have earned a degree as I have."

"I might not have a degree, Gunner, but at least I can still count to five on one hand," Coop said, wiggling the fingers of both complete hands.

"Which is fortunate for you, since you can't count to five *without* your hand."

"Well, what about Wink?" Nita said, her voice raised in an attempt to cut off the volley of insults.

"What *about* the little beast?" Gunner asked.

She eyed the creature warily. He was nestled among the rafters, staring back with the same unbroken, distrustful gaze he had locked on her for the past few days. "Well, Lil said Wink was the newest member of the crew."

"It's actually a cute story. See, that storm wiped out most of the crew, and that included their old inspector. Can't run a ship without one, so the cap'n dipped us down into the northern patch of the fug where they train those things. Something had happened that day. I guess maybe a bunch of the things got in a fight. One of 'em was pretty torn up. Lost an eye and had a bad leg. They were going to kill it. The cap'n wouldn't have any part of it. He demanded to be sold the little guy. He says he was doing it to save money, but believe you me, there was more to it than that. Him and Butch nursed that thing back to health, and to this day I've never seen a more devoted inspector. Until you showed up, the darn thing used to hang around the cap'n any time he wasn't sleeping in the boiler room or doing his inspections. Now he seems to have taken a liking to you. I think he's sweet on you."

Nita glanced at Wink again. "Somehow I don't think that's the reason. What species is it?"

"Oh, heck, I don't know. What about you, college boy?" Coop said.

"It is just an inspector. I only studied things that *matter*."

Wink drummed his fingers. Butch, still stirring a pot, spoke up, though Nita didn't understand a word of it. Instantly Coop and Lil burst into laughter.

"No kiddin'?!" Coop said.

"What?" Nita asked.

"He's called an aye-aye!" Lil snickered.

"Fate does have a sense of humor, don't she?" Coop added. "You reckon we should just call him an *aye* now?"

The ship creaked with a turn, a motion that drew Lil's eyes to the nearest porthole. "Oh, we're coming up on Keystone! Let's get out to the deck, Nita, you're going to want to see this."

Nita and the rest of the crew made their way to the deck, and sure enough, it was a sight she would have been sorry to miss. The continent of Rim was so called because many of its coastal regions were formed by a chain of steep mountains. Along this section of the coast the mountains were narrow and jagged, like the blade of a massive serrated knife. Straddling the peaks of a low section of the mountainside was the city of Keystone, almost surreal in the setting sun. Buildings were built in tiers upon the seaward face of the mountains. Scaffolds and stilts had been built onto the stone, and where the mountain ended, the spindly framework continued, forming a bridge of sorts that served as the base for a bustling community. The buildings were tall and narrow, like the mountains themselves, and smoke and steam belched out of chimneys along the skyline. At the edges of the town where the mountain peaks began to rise up again, the buildings followed. They formed towering and precarious vertical neighborhoods, with long cables ferrying wood and brass cable-trams high over the city, while funiculars were carved into the steepest mountains to carry trains of similar cars down to the main city.

The air around the city was filled with airships. Some were not much larger than the two-man contraptions that had attacked them, while others were practically flying cities, multiple envelopes holding them aloft while dozens of workers scurried across their decks. Mooring towers that were considerably better made than the makeshift contraptions of the Lagomoore Islands rose in regular rows along the very tops of the mountain peaks, extending far beyond the edges of the city, and more occupied long elevated piers that jutted out over the sea.

Perhaps the most wondrous sight of all was what lay beyond the city. Past the taller peaks toward the sea, lesser mountains descended into a second sea. Not more than a few hundred feet below the lowest sections of the city was an endless field of deep lavender haze, whipped by the wind into a swirling, churning mass. It stretched as far as the eye could see, broken only by the occasional island formed by a mountaintop poking through the surface.

"What is it? That field of purple fog?"

"What do you *think* it is? It's the fug. That's what we were left with after the calamity happened all those years ago. That's why what remains of the population of Rim clings to the mountain peaks and plateaus," Gunner said. "We didn't all have a nice, clean chain of islands to hide in when things started to go from bad to worse."

"How far does it go?"

"There isn't much of the continent that doesn't get at least a whiff of the stuff from time to time. It's thickest here where the mountains funnel it up. If you keep your eyes peeled while flying over the heart of the mainland you might catch sight of some stretches of land from time to time, but that's mostly at the whim of the wind and nothing you'd want to risk settling in."

"Where did it all come from?"

"If anyone ever knew that, they died along with most of the rest of us when it first showed up," Coop said. "Alls we know for sure is that it came sudden, rolling in like a tide and catching most low-lying folk by surprise. There weren't as many airships back then. Barely any. The folks who lived were mostly the folks at sea or already in the mountains, or the ones who could get there in a hurry."

"Enough history. There'll be time enough for that later. We'll have to hurry if we're going to be ready in time for our meeting with the fug folk we'll be trading with," Captain Mack said.

Nita watched the implausible urban landscape grow larger as they approached, but slowly something at the edge of hearing drew her attention. It was a tone, pulsing at a quick and irregular rate.

"What *is* that?" she asked.

"What?" Lil asked.

"That sound. It is sort of a ringing sound."

"I don't... *oh.* You mean Wink doing the strut check." She pointed to one of the rigid struts that attached the turbine mounting ring to the deck. Wink had scurried up to the midpoint and was tapping at it vigorously. "He always does a good hard check of that strut when we get close to port. All inspectors do. I reckon, since there is so much steering to do to pull into a dock, they've been trained to check to make sure it's good and strong before we get too close. Shakes the whole envelope, and the sound carries forever. If you listen close, you can probably hear other inspectors doing the same thing on all these other ships. You just start to ignore it after a while."

"I don't remember him doing it on the Lagomoore Islands."

"I reckon even Wink realizes that place ain't no proper port. He mostly does it at the busy spots. Up and down Westrim and Circa, around the edge of the fug, places like that."

"Lil, get Nita down below and find her a mask that fits. She paid us plenty to get her down to talk to those folks personally. I want to make sure she's ready if they allow it."

"Aye, aye, Cap'n," she said. She snickered and added under her breath, "Aye-aye. Don't that beat all?"

Lil took her below decks and led the way to a supply room on deck three. It was filled with canisters and a handful of bizarre masks. They were made from leather and rubber, with copper fittings and a circular vent on the front. Large enough to fit firmly over the mouth, they had long, thin belts to keep them in place.

"Here you go. Try that one on for size," Lil said. "That's the one we keep for guests. Might want to tap it out first. They can get dusty, and the last thing you want is a lungful of dust on your first breath down there."

Nita knocked it against the wall, then held it over her mouth and took a breath. "It is a little hard to breathe with this on," she said. Remarkably, it was well designed enough that it barely muffled her voice at all.

"Not half as hard as it is to breathe without it on once you get down there. It'll sting your eyes a bit, too, but only at first. If that bothers you, Gunner's goggles are good for that. Not yours or mine, though, what with the vents and all. I gotta tell you, I don't envy you going down to talk to those folk. You think Wink can give you the creeps. Every time I see one of those fug folk I feel fit to crawl out of my skin."

"Are they that bad?"

"Heh. You'll see, I guess. Take that with you, get your bag with your payment, and let's go."

Chapter 11

The *Wind Breaker* drifted over the city and moored on the fugward side, facing into an almost mystical scene. Just as was the case on the seaward side, the mountains here were perilously steep, forming almost a sheer drop. The dock rose at the end of a long string of lower hilltops connected by suspension bridges. There, a tall tower with massive iron wheels held wires that led down into the fug. Their berth was as near as possible to the cable tower, just a short walk away from the small building at its base. The crew gathered at the railing beside an embossed sign that had formerly labeled the tram with what looked to be a long and official name. At some point in the past someone had helpfully slathered it with paint reading FUGTOWN EXPRESS.

Captain Mack clicked open his stop watch. "So long as the tram is on time, we'll make it. Coop, the sack."

Coop held out a small canvas bag. "Samples of our wares, and an up-to-date manifest of all available goods."

"We used some on repairs, don't forget."

"Taken into account, Cap'n."

He nodded. "Ms. Graus, are you certain you still want to come along? It won't be pleasant."

"My mother's health depends on this. I want to be sure that everything that can be done will be done," she said.

"Get your mask on then, and make sure you've got everything you brought to trade. I'll talk to the man on the tram, but he'll be expecting you, so the decision will have already been made."

"Did you send a message ahead somehow?"

"They're the fug folk. They'll know. The rest of you, you're on leave for a few hours. Decide among yourselves who stays with the ship and meet back there in two hours. Depending on how this goes, we'll see what's next for us. And if they have any breadfruit at the market, buy a piece for Wink."

The crew didn't wait around to be told twice, vanishing down the catwalk and toward the city proper.

"Now listen closely. It doesn't matter that you hold the purse strings. When it comes to dealing, the fuggers have all the power. Treat these folk as royalty. Speak only when they speak to you. Be respectful. You're as close as your country's ever had to a diplomat to the fug, so you'd best act like it."

"I'll conduct myself properly."

He looked up to the slowly grinding wheel, then checked his watch again. "Sounds like it's close. Say what you want about these folk, they keep to their schedule."

Far below, the purple mist parted and an ornate tram rose out of the fug. It was a work of art, as exquisite as anything Nita might have found in her own land. Looping gold-plated filigree covered the outside. The brass-work was polished to a glorious sheen, and the wood was flawless ebony.

"It's... magnificent."

"What did you expect?"

"Well, from the way you've described them, I expected a ferryman guiding something from the gates of hell."

"Mmm. And who's to say this ain't what that looks like?"

The tram pulled level with the catwalk, and the doors slid open. From inside poured a dense purple fog that swirled about their legs. Even through her leather and canvas leggings, the stuff felt strangely cold. When enough of it drained from within the tram, a man became visible. Nita's breath caught in her chest. He was gaunt, almost skeletal about the face and wrists. His hair was black with streaks of pure white. He wore it slicked back. Every feature of his face was sharp, with a beaklike nose and pronounced cheekbones. His clean-shaven face revealed every deep line in his stoic expression. Every exposed patch of flesh was an ashen-gray color. Thin eyebrows arched haughtily above the most unsettling eyes she had ever seen. The pupils were enormous, easily twice as large as her own, as large as a normal person's iris. Around them, a thin ring of gold bled quickly into orange and then a deep red where the whites should have been. His hands were practically talons, long and slender with bony knuckles and black nails. His spine had a serpentine bend to it, hunching down at the top and swooping forward again at the base. It gave his body the vague shape of a question mark. In contrast to his ghoulish appearance were his clothes. They were as elegant as the tram, made from the finest silk and tailored to fit his twisted body expertly. He wore a black suit jacket with tails. A single black button was fastened, revealing a black silk vest and a white lace ascot. His slacks were straight-cut and led down to black socks and pointed black shoes polished to a glassy finish.

He looked to the two of them, turning first to the captain. "Captain McCulloch West. Punctual as always. A pleasure to be working with you again. Step inside, please." His voice was as sharp and cold as his features. He turned to Nita. "Miss Amanita Graus. It is my great honor to be the first of my people to address a Calderan." He removed a set of white gloves from his pockets and slipped them on before holding out his hand. “Please, let me help you aboard.”

She glanced to the captain, then took the offered hand and stepped aboard. The door slid quietly shut behind her.

“The tram ride will last twenty-seven minutes. As a Calderan, I believe you’ll find the view from this window to be of particular interest.”

She turned to the window, but her heart was fluttering in her chest. Until now, she thought simply stepping onto the *Wind Breaker* had been the most harrowing and dangerous decision she could have made. Since then each day had brought new threats. The strange man had called her by name. No one outside her own homeland should know it, save the members of the crew. How did this fug person learn it?

The tram rumbled into motion, swinging subtly from the wires. It trundled downward, drawing ever closer to the purple mist. Her heart pounded harder with each foot they descended. Then, with a soft whoosh, they plunged into it. The dim light of dusk was wiped away, replaced with pitch blackness. The only light came from the cherry-red glow of the captain’s cigar. The tram operator opened a valve on the wall, and the same sickly yellow glow that lit the lower decks of the *Wind Breaker* filled the tram.

“For your benefit. We of the fug don’t need much light,” he explained.

She felt a strange sensation around her feet and looked down to find that the purple vapor was slipping into the tram, gradually filling it. Captain Mack stubbed out his cigar in an ashtray attached to one wall and cinched his mask in place. Nita tightened the straps on her own. The fug was knee-high now. It felt heavier than the air around it, and where it touched her, it brought the same chill one might get from splashing rubbing alcohol on one’s skin. Her breathing quickened. The fug reached her chest, then her chin. Instinctively she breathed deep and shut her eyes tight when it finally washed over her face. Her eyes burned sharply enough to make them tear.

“The discomfort to your eyes will pass,” their escort said. “You should not feel any lasting effects from exposure to the fug unless you remain immersed for more than forty-eight hours.”

Nita blinked the tears away and looked again to the window. Perhaps it was something the fug had done to her, or perhaps it was simply her vision adjusting, but suddenly she could see a great deal more outside the window. Dull red and green glows pulsed in the field of deep purple.

“The fug is densest in its top layer. Eventually your visibility should reach a mile or so. That glow you see out there is the shipworks. Every airship in the world was built in a facility like that one.”

She stepped closer to the window and squinted. Sure enough, mechanisms and buildings became visible. Unfinished ships with their inner workings exposed drifted through the air. The red glow came from enormous boilers, nearly a match for those back home, but while her own were fueled by the heart of a volcano, these were warmed by massive furnaces that belched fumes and flames. Enormous tubes affixed to pristine envelopes began to swell to shape, spurting puffs of green here and there. Unlike on the surface, where the phlogiston was little more than a bright-green gas, here the stuff was radiant, glowing with the same color as the lights in the tram. Where it sprayed out into the fug, it formed great curling swaths of radiance, like brief but intense tongues of green flame.

Over the next few minutes, Captain Mack sat on one of the plush upholstered seats in the tram while Nita marveled at the otherworldly sights. As they came nearer to the ground, buildings became visible. When they were higher it had been difficult to tell, but now that they were close to the ground it was clear that they had accelerated to a fantastic speed. Street after street whisked by beneath them. It was a whole city, but there was something wrong with it. The streets were empty, lifeless. This wasn't a city built by the fug folk. This was a city that had been strangled by the fug. It was a remnant of whatever people had lived here before, preserved precisely as it had been when the last of them had died away.

"I believe this place was called Duldrum in the days before the calamity. Most of us who live here now can trace ourselves back to the residents who lived here," said their escort.

"You mean you *are* the residents of this place?"

"Indeed. It is true that the fug is *usually* lethal. But some small percentage of the populace doesn't die. We change. We are those blessed by whatever quirk of nature permits such a thing," he said.

"Remarkable..."

"Please take a seat. We will begin to slow now, and it may seem very abrupt."

She did as she was told and was grateful that she did. The tram shuddered and pressed her into her seat, the escort swaying lightly and gripping a handrail for support. They were almost level with the ground now. A loud screech rang out distantly as the brakes on the cable slowed them further, and finally they coasted to a stop. The tram operator opened the door.

"Follow me," he said.

He led the way into the eerie ghost town. The streets stretched out on either side, utterly empty of vehicles, animals, or people. The only sounds were the far-off din of industry and the nearby hiss of a steam engine powering the tram. She knew that a few hundred feet above, the sun was only just setting, but here it seemed to be the dead of night. What light there was came from lamp poles tipped with glass bulbs and glowing with green light. Their destination was the former city hall, a sprawling building, gothic in design, and the only place showing even the remotest sign of activity. He pushed open the door and led them up the stairs to an office labeled, simply, *Mayor.*

"He will see you immediately," said their escort, pushing open the door.

It was a modest office. An old oil lamp provided a warm amber light that seemed far more inviting than the green light elsewhere. Everything was ancient, but exceptionally well cared for, from the elegant antique desk to the stuffed leather chairs that sat two in front and one behind. The walls were book cases, filled with leather-bound tomes of every sort. Sitting behind the desk was another fug person of much the same description, though of somewhat less-formal dress. He reminded Nita of a clerk, with a simple starched white shirt and bow tie. He wore spectacles, and a waxed mustache, jet black against his gray skin, adorned his lip.

"Ah. Captain West. I do so look forward to doing business with you. And this must be the lovely Miss"—he picked up a sheet of parchment and glanced at it, adjusting his glasses—"Amanita Graus. I understand the others call you Nita. I trust you'll do me the honor of affording me the same courtesy."

"Of course."

"Splendid. My name is Mr. Ebonwhite. I oversee all matters dealing with our trade and communication with the people of Keystone. We shall begin with the old business. Captain West, here you will find your outstanding balance." He slid a different parchment forward. "I trust you'll find everything in order."

Mack glanced over the figures and nodded. "Here's our manifest. We've got enough to balance and a fair amount more to trade. We'd like to restore our usual assortment of goods."

"Cheerfully done. We've taken the liberty of preparing your order in advance."

"Thank you. We will also require some repairs."

"Ah, yes. Your encounter with the wailers. We will be happy to oblige. And I must express my relief that Nita here was not injured. It simply would not do for the first Calderan to venture forth in over a century to be killed by a few misguided souls. When you are prepared, send your ship down and we will assess the damage and provide you with a quote for the required service. I understand it will be rather extensive."

"Ms. Graus here would like to ask for a particular item."

"Ah, yes. Something medical if I'm not mistaken."

"I… well, yes. My mother is suffering from a disease. In Caldera it is called Gantt's Disease. It…" She paused as Mr. Ebonwhite looked away to yet another of the many sheets of parchment arrayed on the table.

"Mmm? Oh, I'm sorry, do continue. Something called Gantt's Disease. I'm afraid I'm unfamiliar with it."

"It causes tremors in the fingers. The prognosis is always fatal."

"Mmm… one moment." He stood and approached the far wall, running his fingers along one shelf of books and pulling out a thick tome. He brought it to the table and leafed through. "Uncontrollable trembling… gradual loss of dexterity in the extremities… presents itself when the subject is just exiting middle age."

"Yes, that's it!"

"As fate would have it, that precise disease was a particularly troublesome one for us in the fug. It is caused by an imbalance in the stomach caused by infection. I understand most of those beyond the fug have a natural immunity that we lack. Fortunately a drug we developed, Tomocin, turned out to be quite effective in treating it, as well as a large number of other diseases."

"You can treat the disease?"

"In the case of Moloch's Degenerative Disorder, which is what we call it, the drug is one hundred percent effective. We can cure it. A single course of treatment is enough to permanently eradicate it. Sufferers report a removal of symptoms after a single dose and their complete nonoccurrence after three doses. The disease remains common among us, so we keep a supply on hand."

Nita's heart leapt. "Mr. Ebonwhite, I would gladly pay any price if you would provide me enough of the drug to treat my mother."

"I'm afraid that won't be possible."

"Wh—Why not!"

"Well, if you were a trained diplomat, you would be well aware that there can be no friendly relations between any two nations without the mutual observance of the customs and policies of the other. To be quite frank, you have not respected our ways."

"What did I do?"

"Oh really now, Nita. The repair to the ship's steam system."

The captain's head turned to her. His eyes were almost smoldering with anger.

"I don't know what you are talking about."

"Don't you now? So when Captain West sends his precious *Wind Breaker* down, if we pull up a recently repaired deck board, we won't find that a salvaged connector from a two-seat boarding vessel has mysteriously replaced the one that was fractured when that wailer vessel attacked?"

"Mr. Ebonwhite, I assure you—" the captain began.

"Relax, Captain. We are well aware that you were quite diligent in your warnings, and that Nita took great pains to hide her misdeed from you. These extenuating circumstances have been taken into account, and your resulting fine will be quite mild. You will be charged for the parts and labor to replace the offending part, plus a small fee. Nothing beyond what you can easily pay.

Nita, on the other hand, will need to wait one full year before we are willing to consider trade with her or, indeed, *any* Calderan."

"You—but I—by then my mother will almost certainly have perished."

"A fate that would have befallen her had you not ventured forth from your homeland. It is hardly my concern."

"Please! You can't punish *her* for what *I* did! I admit I disobeyed your rules, but there was a life on the line."

"If it will ease your conscience, I'll inform you that we wouldn't have sold you the drug even if you'd been willing to respect our customs."

"Why?"

"Because there is no profit in it."

"Profit?! But we're talking about life and death here!"

"Yes, Nita. We are. In the fug, profit *is* life and death. You saw our city. There is no sunlight here. That means no crops. Very few animals survived the fug, which means no fresh meat. If we are to survive, we must trade our technology for goods from those on the surface. You are asking for something which will *cure* your mother. That is a single payment. Hardly justifiable."

"There has got to be a better way. I'll pay any price! *Anything*!"

"I have no doubt that you will pay any price, but the simple fact is that you will only ever pay that price once. It would be different if this were a drug that had to be taken again and again, for years and years. The problem is that it is a cure. You'll need it only once, and then you won't need us anymore. We must cultivate our dealings with you and your like as a farmer would a crop. And a crop you can only ever harvest once is no crop at all."

"Surely we can find a way to trade fairly."

"Oh no. There are very few of us, and quite a few of you. *Fair* is unacceptable. It would afford us too little. No, in order for us to survive, the balance *must* be quite heavily in our favor. We trade our disposable goods and, more importantly, our *services*, and we take those steps necessary to ensure that those services will *always* be in high demand."

"How can you be so—?"

"Oh, good heavens, look at the time. I'm terribly sorry, but there are other meetings to prepare for. Captain West, if you'd take your samples to our treasurer for appraisal, we'll settle the additional fees. Nita, you are dismissed. Thank you for your visit, and I do hope to see you again next year, provided you are more willing to behave yourself. Though the treatment you seek is not for sale, I feel certain your people will find we have much else to offer. Good day!"

He plucked a silver bell from the table and tinkled it, summoning the escort to the room, who firmly took Nita's hand and led her out of the office and into the street.

"He can't do this!" she cried as she was pulled with deceiving strength back to the tram.

"He can do whatever he wants. Now shut your mouth before you make things any worse! Go back to the ship. I'll be back in an hour and a half, and we will discuss this matter further."

Her thin escort, nearly crushing her with vicelike fingers that looked as frail as eggshells, herded her into the tram.

"Please! You can't do this! Do you know what I had to do to *get* here?"

"The matter is closed," he said. His tone was gentle, the voice an adult reserves for explaining to a child something that someone so simple could not possibly understand. "It was closed before you arrived. It was closed before we ever knew your name. What you were seeking was never a possibility. I'll send you on your way now. The door will open when you reach Keystone again. Good day, madam."

He pushed her with just enough force to send her backward into the tram, shutting the door before she could recover. And so she was sent on her way. After a few days that had felt like a lifetime, her great gamble had ended in failure in the blink of an eye.

Chapter 12

The ride to the surface was the longest, loneliest time of Nita's life. The weight of all that she'd done, the cold realization of the risks she'd taken and the decisions she'd made, pressed down on her like a lead weight. She had left her life behind, gone where her countryman had wisely chosen and warned her not to go. In doing so, she had taken her life into her own hands... and she'd had a hand in taking the life of another. She'd earned the trust of a group of scoundrels and just as quickly squandered it. Now she was left at their mercy and with nothing to show for it but regret.

By the time the tram broke through the surface of the fug, the sun had finished slipping below the horizon, and the starless night was upon her. She trudged from the tram when it pulled up to the catwalk. The fug poured out around her, exposing her to fresh air once more. The mountain air was cool, but compared to the chemical chill of the fug, it was almost muggy. She pulled free her mask and, for the first time, caught an unfiltered whiff of the stuff that still clung to her clothes. It was horrid, overpowering. She could compare it to nothing in her life to date. Somewhere between strong solvents and burning weeds, but each to a depth and scale that almost caused her to retch.

She wandered back to the closest thing she had to a home for thousands of miles, the trusty *Wind Breaker*, and climbed aboard. Her feet had barely touched the rungs of the dangling ladder when the distinctive sound of a gun cocking came from above. She looked up to see Gunner, apparently the one who'd drawn the short straw and remained behind to defend the ship.

"Ms. Graus. I'd suggest you announce yourself next time," he said, easing down the hammer of the pistol. It was yet another fresh one from his collection, this one with a flared end and a barrel as wide as that of a shotgun.

"I'm sorry," she muttered, continuing up the ladder. "And you may as well call me Nita."

"Oh? Why the change of heart?"

"Because I think your first impression of me was a sound one. I was a liability after all."

"I don't know about that," he said, lending a hand and hauling her up the last few rungs. "You've proved to be versatile, at the very least."

"Perhaps too much so."

"You didn't."

She nodded slowly.

"Where? I scoured that boiler! Nothing had changed!"

"It was up on the deck. I didn't… I…"

Gunner's fingers tightened at the grip of his weapon, and he slowly eased the hammer back again. "Where is the captain?" He uttered the words almost as a demand, as though Nita was holding the captain hostage somewhere.

"He's still talking to them."

Her crewmate's face was a mask combining concern and fury.

"What happens now?" she asked.

"What happens now is I make damn sure that you don't go *anywhere* or touch *anything* until he comes back."

"You aren't going to kill me, are you?"

"I won't do *anything* I'm *not* ordered to do, and I will do *everything* I *am* ordered to do. Because that is what a crew does. It obeys its captain."

Over the next hour, the crew returned one at a time, calling out to Gunner and climbing into the gig room to find Nita at gun point. The looks in their eyes were like daggers to her heart, but what hurt most was that not a single one of them needed to be told what was happening, nor what had happened. They'd expected this from her, regardless of what they hoped. The only one who spoke was Lil, and only a single word.

"Why?" The word wouldn't have sounded any different if she'd spoken it with a knife sticking out of her back.

Almost precisely two hours from when the first tram had picked up Nita and the captain, the final tram dropped him off. He climbed the ladder to find Gunner and Nita still in the gig room.

"I am going to my quarters," he said. "Nita, follow me. The rest of you will have your orders soon enough."

Nita took the long walk to Captain Mack's quarters in silence. When they reached the door he pulled it open and marched inside. She stepped in after him, and before she closed the door Wink hopped through and scampered up to his net hammock. The captain eased into his seat.

"Sit," he said.

"Captain, I—"

"Sit down and hold your tongue. I'll speak to you when I'm ready, and until I do, you will keep quiet. I want answers and nothing else. There ain't nothing to defend. These are orders, Ms. Graus. Long past time you started following them."

He fished a fresh cigar out of its jar and lit it, finally chasing away the chemical stench of the fug that still faintly clung to him. After two more contemplative puffs he blew out a cloud of black cherry smoke.

"It was at the Lags," he said. "When it was you and Lil. That's when you did it. You looked me in the eye and you lied." He puffed again. "There's something to be admired there. Ain't no one but the missus put one past me like that in a dog's age." Another puff. "Tell me. Did you think about what this would mean for Lil?"

"Lil had nothing to do with it."

"Oh, she did. You were her responsibility. Didn't think of that, I take it? Not surprised. Doesn't seem to me you do a lot of thinking when it doesn't suit your ends."

"Captain, it was a mistake—"

"A mistake. That's what you call a mistake in Caldera, is it? You repaired something you were ordered not to. You lied to me and my entire crew. You tinkered with this ship, which is our livelihood and may as well be our lives, and you did it because you believed after just a few hours among us that you knew better than any of us how *our* world worked. That's not what I call a mistake. That's what I call arrogance. Irresponsible, childish arrogance. It's cost me a dear price, and I mean to see it does the same to you."

"What did the fug folk demand of you?"

He took another slow drag on the cigar and released it with a breath. "Everything. They knew how much we had, and with the usual fleecing they give us plus the cost of the repairs and the 'small' fine for your disobedience, that leaves us flat busted. They didn't ruin us. You don't slaughter a sheep for its wool, but everything we done for the last few years has been for nothing."

"I'm so sorry. Captain, I promise you, when we return to Caldera I'll give you everything you need to replace what was lost."

"You presume an awful lot to suggest you'll get the opportunity. Some debts can't be paid with a pile of coins. Some debts require blood."

Nita took a deep breath. "You seem to be a reasonable man, Captain. What would blood solve?"

"It would make an example of you, Ms. Graus. This is a ship. I don't give a damn about how many minds a ship has, but it can only have one will. The will of the captain. Right or wrong, I can't have disagreement. You saw it during the wailer attack. We work as one, toward one goal. If there is doubt or dissension, the ship will fall apart."

He puffed at his cigar for a few more moments.

"So what will you do?" she asked.

"I ain't decided yet, and you don't want to rush me. Not so soon after dealing with the fug folk. Them folks boil my blood."

"May I ask you a question?"

"Seems you might not have too many more chances. May as well."

"Do you follow their rules because you want to or because you have no choice?"

"I got no problem with following the rules of people I respect… but that ain't the case with these folk. They got us under their thumbs, and they know it. You think it's bad what they're willing to do to your mother? That ain't the half of it. They've sat idle while whole cities starved because their ships were too beat-up to pick up supplies, and the fuggers wouldn't budge on the price of repairs. They've choked off shipments of coal to places in northern Circa because they found out the locals were mining their own seam to top off their supplies. The fuggers demand reliance and will punish anything that threatens it. Most times I'd say they want profit above all else, but sometimes it seems to me they want one thing even more. Power. Letting your mother die. Letting them folks in them cities die… They throw away plenty of good business just to make sure we know who's in charge. If I could get out from under them, I'd… well, best not to say what I'd do."

"So it all comes down to whoever has been giving them their information."

"No one is telling them. They just know. And you aren't earning any points suggesting one of my crew would have ratted the rest out."

"I apologize. I suppose there wasn't any member of the crew to see what *I* did either… except…" She turned her eyes to Wink. The creature huddled backward under her glare. Her mind began to flood with days of observations slowly connecting. "Captain, when they gave you the figure of what you'd owe, did they include what I had in my bag?"

"The pendant and the trith coil. What I'd included as your intended payment."

"But not anything else?"

"No."

"Why not? Surely if they knew you had it to spend they would have required that of you as well. Particularly knowing that it was *my* property, that of the perpetrator."

"What are you getting at?"

"They didn't ask for it because they didn't know about it. I seldom let the bag out of my sight. None of the crew knew how much I had." She opened the bag and pulled out the full-size coil box, slamming it on his desk. "This is made mostly out of trith. Unless I'm wrong, this should have been worth more than any single thing on the ship. If they just magically knew things, they would have demanded it, wouldn't they?"

The captain didn't answer immediately, his mind briefly preoccupied by the immense wealth that had just been dropped in front of him. "This was what you were going to use to pay for the drug?"

"If they would have given me the chance."

"I don't know a fug person who wouldn't step over his own mother to get that much trith."

"So they clearly don't simply *know* things. Someone must be telling them."

"But no member of my crew would ever do that."

"How much do you know about Wink and his kind?"

"What's to know? He's an inspector. Maybe not the best, but the best one I've had."

"But how intelligent are they?"

"Intelligent enough to take a simple order and to know a good board from a bad one."

"What if they were smarter than that?" Wink dropped down to the floor and hopped to the door, attempting to haul it open. Nita braced it shut with her foot. "I said that there was no one to see me do the repair, but Wink was there the whole time, watching me. He's been watching me since I arrived." Now Wink started to chew at the door, chisel-like teeth carving easily into the wood. "And he seems to be awfully interested in getting away now that I've started talking about his potential treachery."

The captain stood, leaned across his desk and caught the creature by the tail, raising it up and dropping it to the desk, where his other hand held it.

"I'll allow that he's acting a mite odd at the moment, but smart as he might be, the little thing can't talk, and even if he could, he never meets the fug folk face-to-face. They have me take him off the ship when we send it down for repairs."

"You don't need to speak—or even meet face-to-face—to communicate, Captain. Back in the steamworks, we worked out a tap code to hammer out messages along the pipes. Wink does something awfully similar whenever you get close to the fug, doesn't he?"

"The strut check..." He looked down to the beast. For the first time, genuine fear replaced the vague distrust in its eye. The captain held Wink's pelt tight and stood him up. "Let's just test this. I'll make it simple for you.

One tap for yes, two for no. Do you want me to give you to Glinda to see what sort of stew she could make of you?"

The creature's head darted back and forth, looking the two humans in the eye. It was telling enough that he wasn't frantically tapping his fingers as he usually did when something had him agitated. He struggled a bit more, then seemed to give up. He extended his spidery middle finger and gave two deliberate taps.

"Have you been the one telling the fug folk about us?"

Wink's head and ears drooped. *Tap.*

"You little piece of filth!"

"It makes perfect sense. The fug folk *require* all airships to have one, and since they are inspectors, they get free run of the ship," Nita said.

The captain was still preoccupied with the revelation. "I saved your *life*! They were going to give you the knife. You are a member of my *crew.*"

The little beast was the picture of shame. *Tap.*

"Look at me. Look at me!"

Wink reluctantly faced him.

"You will never, *never* report on this ship again. Understand?"

Tap.

"And will you report on us again?"

Tap, tap.

"I ain't through with you, but I've got other things need discussing. You get back there and sit down!"

Wink obeyed, climbing up to the hammock and continuing to wear the most heart-wrenchingly forlorn face Nita had ever seen.

"I think—" Nita began, but the captain's eyes were distant.

It was clear that the revelation of how he'd been watched had brought with it a flood of opportunities to his mind. In short order, he seemed to come to a decision.

"You would do anything to get them drugs for your mother?"

"Yes."

"And you're serious about making things square with us for what you done?"

"I am."

"Well… what I got in mind ain't quite enough to make us square. You'd still have a punishment coming, but if this is going to work I'd need you working pretty near nonstop for the next few days. Tell me, you want a bit of payback against them fuggers?"

She flashed a devilish smile. "I do."

He leaned down and pulled a bottle and two glasses from a low cupboard. He placed them down and poured a splash of strong-smelling brown liquor into each.

"I really don't drink that sort of—"

"Ms. Graus, there are some conversations that can't be had properly without a pair of strong drinks in hand." He handed her a glass. "You and I are about to have one." He settled back in his chair. "The fug folk will never sell you that medicine. That just leaves you the one way to get it."

"You're proposing we steal the medicine?"

"Not just the medicine, Ms. Graus. The toys and trinkets they let us buy to spread around are nothing compared to what they keep for themselves. There isn't a day that's gone by I haven't thought of it. Every time they smacked me down with a new rule or tax or fee. I've thought about it plenty. I've been to the storehouses. I've seen what they have."

"They let you see where they store their valuables?"

"Some of them, anyway. And why shouldn't they? Until now, if anyone were to even discuss this sort of thing, their little spies would have passed along a warning. The good news is what Mr. Ebonwhite said was true. There aren't many fug folk. The storehouses aren't well guarded, but they *are* well defended. They've got some mighty deadly gadgets. Not only that, but these are the people who make the airships. Believe it when I tell you, they keep the best for themselves. But I think this crew has what it takes to pull it off, because we've got the one thing they never expected anyone to have: surprise." He puffed his cigar. "Of course, the thing to remember is that once we do this, that'll be it for my dealings with the fug folk. At least the sort of dealings where we aren't trying to kill each other."

"So no more trading goods… and no more repairs."

"You said you could fix this ship. And you showed you could. You figure you can get the whole steam system patched up in two days?"

"With some help, I think so."

"Well, all right. Here's the long and short of it, then. If you really want to get that medicine, and you want to make up for what you done, then I think we can storm the gates and make out like proper bandits. But in exchange, you'll need to stay on as my engineer at least until you can train the others to do what needs doing. What do you say?"

It was an enormous question, likely the most important one she would ever face. In just a few days outside of her home she'd been thrust into situations far beyond her control. She'd nearly been killed, and she'd watched herself slip further and further toward a person she'd hoped never to become. He was offering her both the final step toward becoming a lawless scoundrel and the chance to both redeem herself in their eyes and gain what she'd traded so much of her innocence to attain. It was a question that warranted hours of contemplation, days even. Instead, her answer came with the next breath.

"When do we start?"

He smiled and held up his glass. She clinked hers to it and both drank. The victorious moment was spoiled somewhat by her sudden and violent coughing fit. He laughed.

"This stuff is really something, huh? My brother makes it. Got a bit of a broken-glass front end. Maybe a poison-ivy finish?" He grimaced a bit and puffed on his cigar. "I used to have a bit of a drinking problem. That's when my brother gave me this stuff. It was so awful I couldn't stand a second swallow. I figured stocking nothing but a few bottles of this was a good way to avoid pickling myself. I do still soak my cigars in black-cherry brandy though. What can I say? A man needs a vice. Now go. Gather the crew. We'll figure out what needs to be done." He turned to his hammock. "I'll have a word with the spy."

Chapter 13

Nita stood at the prow of the airship, recovering from the past few hours of work, as the sun set two days later. It would have been nice to suggest that much of the preceding forty-eight hours had been spent sketching out a detailed and nuanced plan. Such was not the case. The entirety of their brilliant plan came in the form of the captain announcing, "We'll drop down when we're scheduled for repair, hit them fast, take anything it looks like they don't want us to take, and if anyone tries to stop us, we'll discourage that." The rest of the time had been spent preparing the ship for the worst.

For Coop and Lil, that meant scouring the ship and the local supply houses for all of the wood and envelope material they could get their hands on, first to repair and then to reinforce the gondola hull. They slopped a layer of tar onto the envelope to provide a measure of self-sealing, then stitched on an extra layer of material in the most vulnerable spots. Glinda had made a few trips to Keystone's market district to stock up on medical supplies in expectation of casualties. The captain spent his time testing various repairs and literally keeping Wink on a short leash. Now that the little scoundrel's secret had been discovered, it quickly became clear that he was far more intelligent than anyone had suspected. Whether it was out of genuine shame or simple self-preservation, the aye-aye had proved himself quite willing to render whatever aid he could.

With the rest of the crew otherwise occupied, that left the most crucial aspect of the preparations to Nita and Gunner. Their time was entirely devoted to reconfiguring the boiler into something fully functional and adding in some other accessories. Gunner, after some initial reluctance, grew rather enthusiastic about the endeavor.

"So this valve keeps the pressure from reaching the pipe you're repairing, right? And this chamber builds the pressure?"

"Yes."

"Well, this boiler nonsense isn't so hard after all. It is just heat and pressure. Not so different from a bomb, really. Just a bit slower."

"Once again, I wish you would stop comparing the boiler to something that is supposed to explode. Explosions are what we are trying to avoid."

"If I'm ever going to bridge my skills, I'll need to start from some common ground."

"Just so long as you don't start getting them confused," Nita said. She applied a torch and some solder to a final permanent joint and stepped back. "Turn on that valve and let's see how it holds." He did so, and after a shudder and hiss failed to reveal any leaks, she brushed off her hands. "That's everything."

The repairs had consumed almost every piece of the salvaged wailer, and they had repurposed many of the seemingly needless odds and ends that the fug folk had included. She looked over the pressure gauges.

"It isn't pretty, and we're running a little lower on pressure than we were when it was purely as designed by the fug folk. Maybe two notches, but I'll bet with a bit of tuning we can get that back. I'd also like to do some firmer connections down in the—"

"If you stay on this ship long enough, you'll learn that pursuing perfection does nothing but steal time from things that desperately need work. The policy of this ship is 'Good enough is good enough.' You try to do any better than that and—"

The captain's voice bellowed over the speaking tube: "Time is up. I'm seeing full pressure on the turbines. It is time to head out. Coop, Lil, lines in."

"You see? Now, mask on, and stay below deck."

The *Wind Breaker* shuddered and pulled away from the dock. Nita and Gunner moved out to the hall and found their way to the nearest porthole. It was strange, but listening to the turbines above hum with the healthy rhythm she'd heard when they first left filled her with a flash of pride. After only a few days, she'd come to feel rather protective of the little ship. It had already been responsible for the greatest adventure of her short life, though the next hour was likely to eclipse every danger that had come before.

Captain Mack took the ship into a steep dive, plunging quickly down into the fug. It flushed through the ship, forcing itself through cracks between boards and belching through hatches and halls. A wave of purple fumes rushed over them, instantly stinging their eyes and chilling their skin. Nita looked closer to the porthole, her heart beginning to pound. There was nothing but darkness. Even after the dense surface of the fug was above them, there was nothing to see. The captain must have selected a route that would keep them far from any of their facilities and structures.

"I've had to stay with the ship once or twice during repair runs," Gunner said. "It's a shortest-straw sort of situation. They only allow ships to come down for handing over goods, picking up goods, and getting repairs. All three are handled by the Fugtown Lower Docks, over on the other side of town. We're not supposed to be here. There *will* be patrols."

"What happens if they see us?"

"Then the shooting starts early."

"How does the captain plan to avoid them?"

"The captain doesn't plan. He just dives in."

She smirked. "I *thought* there was something about him that seemed familiar. I do the same thing."

"So I've noticed."

The thump of footsteps came from above, then Coop and Lil joined them in the hall. Lil was rubbing at her eyes.

"Hoo-wee. I forgot how much that smarts. This is only the second time I been in the fug, you know," she said. "Last time was back when Cap'n Mack rescued us."

She was still rubbing her eyes when she came upon Nita in the narrow hallway, bumping into her.

"Sorry, I—" She looked up. Her face hardened a bit. "Oh, it's you."

Aside from the initial gathering of the group to announce the plan, Lil and Nita had been kept apart by their duties, but even so it had been clear that she felt a good deal more betrayed than the rest. Gunner glanced up to see the tension between the two of them. He then turned to see Coop picking at his ear and generally being oblivious to the pregnant silence.

"Coop," Gunner said. "Maybe you and I should go down to the gig room."

"What for?" he asked, digging a little deeper and rolling his eyes in something between ecstasy and irritation.

"Just come with me, you oaf," Gunner said, snagging his arm.

The two men vanished down the hall. Lil crossed her arms.

"You gonna apologize?" she asked.

"Will it do any good?" Nita replied.

"Worth a shot."

"I wasn't thinking about you or anyone else. I just wanted to do what I could to save my mother, and I ended up doing something foolish, disrespectful, and wrong."

"And you did it on *my* watch."

"Yes. I'm sorry for all of it. I don't know if it is forgivable, and frankly I won't dare expect you to forgive me. We've got a big job to do right now, though, and so if you can't accept my apology, perhaps we can at least call a truce."

Nita held out her hand. Lil looked at it thoughtfully, then knocked it aside. "Aw heck. Truces and handshakes are for politicians and such. Come here." She threw her arms around Nita and gave her a hug, thumping her on the back before stepping away. "You did something stupid that you thought you'd get away with. I of all people can't fault you for that. And the way I figure it, no matter how low he busts me, I was already at the bottom of the ladder before you showed up, and he's gonna *have* to bust you lower, so we're back where we left off. I ain't got time to stay mad anyway. We got a job to do that could kill us. I'd hate to go to my grave holding a grudge. So I'll forgive you, but on two conditions."

"What are they?"

"First, you gotta let me try that dress on."

Nita smiled. "Tough but fair."

"And second, don't you go doing something stupid like that again."

"Of course not. We've got a much stupider situation to deal with."

"You're darn right, so let's get to it."

#

The *Wind Breaker* drifted low to the ground, nearly brushing the tops of the buildings that made up the sprawling and deserted cityscape. This far from the active part of the city there were no lamps to light the way. Captain Mack was forced to navigate by the dim glow of two large phlo-lights built into the prow. Combined with the low visibility, it was more a matter of luck than skill that they hadn't been dragged across the spire of a particularly tall building, but not a whisper of concern showed on his face. The captain stood firm at the helm, the wind rustling his hair. Wink languished at the end of a short length of rope. He wore a hastily fashioned harness and had his eye trained on the darkness ahead. As a creature of the fug, he breathed well enough in the stuff. Even with only one eye, his vision was sharper than any other crewmember in the darkness, to say nothing of his hearing.

"You let me know the instant you see or hear something besides the wind, you understand?" Captain Mack said.

Tap.

"Good. You see us through this, and you just might still have a place in this crew."

Wink twitched his batlike ears and angled them, then drummed his claws and pointed. The captain squinted. Just barely visible in the indicated direction glowed similar ship lights. He leaned low and spoke into the communication tube.

"We're getting close. If you aren't in the gig room, get there. I'm going to drop you off due south of the warehouse district. When you've got as much as you're going to get, send up one of the flares. I'll bring the *Wind Breaker* in and we'll hightail it, but be ready to load in a hurry. Glinda and the traitor will stay with me to man the ship."

"How do we know we're almost there, Cap'n?" came Coop's voice. "I can't hardly see anything."

"You'll see it in a minute, if you keep your eyes starboard. Our inspector spotted a patrol. I don't reckon they'd waste their time on any old corner of the city. Time to get their attention. Brace yourselves. This'll be rough."

The captain removed the linking bars for the various control levers and began to push them apart. The turbines groaned against their mountings and twisted the ship into an odd, diagonal drift. One of the turbines started to bind, producing a terrible whining noise. He eased the misaligned throttle just a bit to cut the sound off, but it had done its job. The patrol was on its way.

Unlike the patchwork and much abused *Wind Breaker*, the patrol ship was sleek and pristine as it emerged from the darkness. A grid of green lights was affixed to each side of its prow, and a line of fléchette guns and grapplers similar to those used by the wailers was mounted to the forward railing. The only thing the *Wind Breaker* had on it was size, as the craft was barely a third as large and manned by only three people.

"Attention!" announced one of the crewmembers, bellowing through a megaphone. "This section of Fugtown is restricted. If you have business here, be prepared to present your authorization. Otherwise return to the docks."

"Oh, I've got business all right," Captain Mack called out as best as he could through his mask. "I'm supposed to be getting this crate repaired. Only problem is, the damn thing started to drift on me. Got way off course. I'd be glad to take a tow, if you're offering."

"If you are in distress, why didn't you sound your distress whistle?"

"Been busted for even longer than the turbines."

The crew of the patrol ship conferred. Captain Mack didn't show a flicker of concern. The same could not be said for Wink. From the moment the fug folk had come into view he had been trying to hide behind the captain. After a brief discussion, one crewman manned a grappler, and another stepped to a gun.

"There is a courtyard a quarter of a mile east of here. Guide your ship there, power down, and drop anchor. Once we confirm that you are immobile, we will leave a man with you and send for a dedicated tow ship. In the future, report for repair before your ship is so severely disabled."

"I'll do my best, but finances are none too obliging." He leaned low and spoke as quietly as was reasonable into the speaking tube. "When the anchor drops, so do you. The dragging anchor should cover your noise."

#

Above, the captain maneuvered his ship with apparent difficulty into the courtyard. The portion of the crew representing the away team watched through the open personnel hatch as the dimly lit ground slid by. Each crewmember was loaded down with whatever equipment they felt they might need, along with as many empty sacks as they could carry, and they'd tied additional equipment into bundles and chained it along the length of a rope.

Captain Mack angled the ship such that the hatch was in shadow, giving them the maximum cover but minimum visibility. He then lowered the ship dangerously close to the ground and prepared the seldom-used anchor.

"We go one at a time. Standard land evacuation methods."

"Wait. I don't *know* the standard land evacuation methods," Nita said.

"He just means jump. And try to roll when you hit the ground," Coop said. "Hope it doesn't bust my stitches."

"This sounds like the sort of thing I should have practiced," Nita said.

"No time like the present!" Lil said. The frightening sound of the anchor dropping onto the cobblestone of the courtyard rang out. "Follow my lead, and make sure you don't lose your mask!"

Lil braced her mask to her face with one hand and dropped through the hatch, plummeting five or six feet. She landed feet first, pitching forward into a shoulder roll and ending up on her feet and running. Coop kicked the bundles of equipment out, then followed them. He didn't have quite the same level of grace, but he nonetheless landed without a scratch. Next, it was Nita's turn. She held her mask tight and jumped.

Coop and Lil had made it look easy, but it wasn't until she was in the air that Nita realized if there was a knack to it, she hadn't worked it out. She hit the ground hard, tipping forward into more of a tumble than a roll. When she finally slid to a stop she was a bit bruised, a few of her tools went clattering across the ground, and her ankle made a worrying crack, but she was still in one piece.

Lil made her way to Nita at a low run, helping her to her feet and gathering her lost tools. The three of them snagged the fallen equipment bundle.

Gunner opted for a different exit, dangling down from the edge by his hands to shorten his fall. His plan was somewhat foiled when the anchor finally bit into the courtyard, causing a sudden and violent end to the *Wind Breaker*'s drift and dislodging him before he was ready. He fell to the ground and landed hard on his back. Despite only falling a few feet, he seemed utterly shocked.

"You okay, Gunner?" Lil whispered as she and Nita helped him to his feet.

"Easy, easy," he said insistently.

"Oh, calm down. It was barely a fall. I jumped *twice* as far as you, and you don't see me getting all twitchy."

"But *you* aren't strapped with firearms and explosives."

"Good point."

"Quit fooling around back there," Coop said. "Let's get moving before they notice us down here."

The group moved as swiftly and silently as they could, heading due north. Once they were out of the dim halo of light cast by the ships, they found themselves stumbling in inky blackness. Only the remote glow of a second ship far in the distance broke up the tapestry of midnight purple around them. The heavy, dense fumes seemed to deaden sound as well, swiftly muting the noise of the ships and leaving them with nothing but their own footsteps and labored breaths. When she felt they were far enough to escape notice, Nita pulled her trusty gas lamp from her belt and sparked it to life. The group huddled around the circle of light.

"Who's got the compass?" she asked.

"Right here," Coop said. He pulled it out. "We're headed in the right direction."

"Are we sure? I can't see anything. This place is pitch black. I don't know how he could possibly navigate down here."

"Trust me when I tell you, the cap'n could make the whole trip to Caldera and back with his eyes closed. He wouldn't be the cap'n otherwise."

"Well, let's keep moving north then," Nita said. "Everyone keep your eyes peeled for something it looks like they don't want us to break into."

#

"I thought that anchor would never dig in," Captain Mack called out, regaining his footing after the sudden stop.

"Stand clear," the patrolman ordered. "We will send over two grapplers. Secure them and I will send a chaperone aboard."

The patrolman manning the grappling-hook launcher fired off a hook, then loaded and fired another. Captain Mack made sure they were hooked onto something sturdy, and the patrol ship winched out the slack and hauled the gondolas close enough to bridge the gap with a gangplank. One of the scrawny men scurried across. He was dressed similarly to the others in a gray vaguely military uniform, including a long jacket and a cap with a short brim. Armed with a long rifle, he held it at the ready, as though he were venturing into enemy territory. Mack offered him a hand to help him down to the deck, but the patrolman sneered at it with smug disdain.

"We shall return with a tow. There will of course be a fee involved," the superior officer announced from the patrol ship as he pulled back the gangplank and his subordinate aboard the *Wind Breaker* unhooked the grapplers.

"Can't imagine there wouldn't be," Mack called back. "You folk do seem to find a way to charge for damn near everything."

If the officer had heard the jab, he made no indication. Instead he took the controls of his ship and steered it off toward the center of Fugtown. Mack turned to the chaperone. The fug person was eyeing the ship with the trained suspicion of someone who expected nothing less than murderous treachery at the root of any given interaction.

"This ship looks like it's been recently patched," he said. "What are those?"

He indicated two sections of railing that were wrapped and tied with blankets. Each bulged up beneath its covering.

"Telescopes. We take folks on sightseeing trips. Wasn't sure if the fug would be good for 'em, so we trussed 'em up. You'd be surprised how sensitive those things can—"

"Why is your inspector wearing a harness?"

"He's been up to things he shouldn't be up to. Thought it was wise to keep him where I could see him. No telling what sort of hijinks—"

"If it isn't performing its duties, you should have it replaced. It is clearly damaged."

"He might be a handful sometimes, but he's still been part of the crew for a while. I think he can be straightened out. You want any food while we're waiting? My cook's still on board, and she's the best in Keystone."

"Certainly not," he said with the same revulsion as if he'd been offered a raw pig head to eat. "I am here to ensure you don't do anything foolish. I don't want any of your horrid swill, and I don't want to hear about what you use this broken-down ship to do." He pointed the rifle at the captain. "Just keep quiet until then, and this assignment will at least be tolerable."

"If that's the way you want it to be," Captain Mack said. He turned to watch the patrol ship retreating, then pulled a half-smoked cigar from his pocket and idly twirled it through his fingers. "A word of advice though, if you ever find yourself on my ship again."

"What insipid advice could you possibly give me?"

"Don't insult my ex-wife's cooking."

"I will do whatever I—"

A heavy clang cut his statement short as Butch delivered a punishing blow to the back of his head with a meat tenderizer. The blow was enough to send him to the ground in a dazed stupor. She growled a vicious, unintelligible statement and spat.

"Sometimes I wonder why we ever separated, darlin'. I'll tie him up. You keep an eye out for that flare." He knelt beside their prisoner and got to work. "The fella is going to have a very interesting bruise to remember this by."

#

The away team had made it to the edge of the courtyard. Overhead, the worrying drone of a second patrol ship loomed. Around them sprawled a "neighborhood" of neglected buildings. It was the first unsupervised look any of them had seen of what the fug had left behind, and it troubled them in a profound way. When a war sweeps through a place it leaves the city in ruins, broken and unlivable. Such was not the case here. Though many of the buildings were beginning to suffer from lack of maintenance, some looked perfect. If she'd not known the truth, Nita could have imagined a bustling community making its home here just days ago. A sense that all of the people had simply vanished, leaving their world behind, lingered.

Nita took in what she could see of their surroundings. They were walking along the edge of what had probably been the main road of the area. Unlike the artful architecture of her own home, the buildings were boxy and utilitarian. Some were multistory homes, but as they moved on, most were stout and sprawling structures, factories perhaps, or warehouses. They'd been built simply and efficiently from masonry, but everything had an unnaturally dark tint. The fact that everything, from the shingles to the iron fences, and even the withered trees, had the same tint suggested that the fug was to blame.

The droning of turbines grew louder, and the dim green light of a ship cast a long shadow.

"Come on, let's get to the alley. We're far enough from the main city that any motion at all will give us away," Gunner said.

They huddled together in the long, tall space between two warehouses and waited for the ship to pass by. The patrol ship seemed to coast to a stop above them, its green light painting a stark line across the ground, forcing them farther back into the shadows. Finally the turbines revved, and the ship moved on.

"We *gotta* be close now. That ship is lingering right around this spot," Coop said.

Lil squinted in the distance. "What's that at the other end of the alley? Across the other courtyard there."

Gunner, pulled a rifle from his back and raised it, peering through the scope.

"I can just barely make it out through this pea soup. It looks like a single guard, lightly armed, standing in front of a well-lit door," he said.

"That's got to be the place. Let's go. Everyone know their parts?" Nita asked.

"Lil and I take out the fugger all quiet like, then you and Gunner get the door open. After that, we take everything we can carry," Coop said.

"This is gonna be fun! We'll signal you by shutting off the light," Lil added.

With that, the two siblings sprinted silently down the alley. Nita and Gunner followed far behind.

"Is this the sort of thing you do often?" Nita asked.

"No, attempting to rob the people who supply the entirety of our technology is uncharted territory for us."

"The Coopers seem awfully at ease with it."

"Those two haven't got the brain power to do anything but live in the moment. Working out the consequences or dangers of a given action takes too much effort. Sometimes I envy them," Gunner said. "You'd think it would make them poor workers, but when you've only got mind enough to have a single train of thought, you have no choice but to throw yourself entirely into it."

"I'm not certain if you're trying to insult them or compliment them."

"Merely observing. You can sort the rest out yourself."

#

The guard took a deep breath of the chilly air and tightened his jacket. He always hated when he pulled guard duty. It was utterly pointless. In six years of guard duty the most action he'd seen was when some shingles blew off the roof during a storm. Every night was the same: standing on this old wooden landing beside a reinforced door, a barred window, and a flickering phlo-lamp, quietly listening to his pocket watch tick away the hours until one of the patrol ships stopped to drop off his replacement. He heaved a sigh and turned to the window, adjusting the brightly colored ascot that he'd added to his otherwise drab uniform. That, at least, was the nice thing about guard duty. No one with the authority to reprimand him ever came out this far, so he was free to take some dress-code liberties.

A skittering stone caught his attention and he turned, reaching for his gun. There was nothing to be seen, just the same empty stretch of courtyard that filled his view every night. He turned back and leaned side to side, trying to get a full reflection of himself in the glass behind the bars.

"Still looks a bit crooked if you ask me," Lil said.

The man panicked, reached for the rifle again, and found it missing. He turned to the source of the voice and swiftly discovered that his rifle hadn't gone far. It was now in the hands of a skinny surface-dwelling girl with a mischievous gleam in her eye. He gasped and tried to call for help, but before he could utter a syllable a hand covered his mouth.

"What's the matter, fella? You never done this before?" Coop asked. "See, when someone points a gun at you, you keep quiet. Chances are, the only reason they didn't pull the trigger is because they didn't want to make a ruckus and draw any attention. If you go and draw attention yourself, they may as well shoot. Now I'm going to ask you for the key to this here door. And if you do anything but answer quietly, I'm gonna have to bust your neck, and I never done that before, so it might take a few tries. I don't reckon that'll be too comfortable for you. You understand?"

He nodded.

"So." Coop removed his hand and stepped in front of the guard. The fug person was typically tall and thin, making him the rare individual that Coop had to look up to talk to, if only slightly. "Where's the key?"

"Don't have the key. The quartermaster has the key, and he only comes here to pick up and drop off shipments," the man said desperately, adding, "Please don't kill me!"

"Well, see, you ain't got the key, so you really aren't that useful to us. Say…" Coop grabbed the ends of the ascot. "What do you call this thing?"

"It's an ascot," he said.

"What's it for?"

"Well, it's for being all fancy like, obviously," Lil said.

"That ain't what *I'd* use it for," Coop said.

"What else could you use it for?" she asked.

He replied with a demonstration, using it to yank the man's head down and pulling it into a powerful head butt that sent him to the ground.

"I s'pose that's more of a reason *not* to wear one," Lil said.

"That's what I was trying to show off."

"Well, then you done a good job. Not so much for this fella, though. I guess he'll get the point when he wakes up." She stepped over the unconscious man and twisted off the flow for the light. "I like his gun, though."

Nita and Gunner hurried across the darkened courtyard.

"Psst, Gunner," Lil hissed when he was near enough to hear. She held up the gun. "Jealous?"

"Put that down. Make yourself useful and scout the area for other guards while we get the door open," he growled.

Lil saluted. "Will do."

Once again, with disturbing silence, she vanished into the darkness, Coop hot on her heels.

"Okay, let's see what we have here," Nita said, eyeing up the door and turning up the flame on her gas lamp.

Unlike the rest of the building, which was a fairly simple (albeit very large) brick warehouse, the door looked like something from a vault. Thick iron bars ran through heavy braces on either side and were connected in the center to a massive gear with easily the most complex lock Nita had ever seen. There were three keyholes interlinked with rods and cogs, and other gears connected the central one to a series of smaller braces up and down the sides of the door. The lock seemed to hold in place two smaller rods that ran up from the base of the door and down from the top, preventing the gear from turning.

"This looks like trouble," Gunner said. "I suppose I'll get the explosives."

Nita looked closer at the locking bars and gave them a tap with a wrench. "It looks like these are the only things we'll have to overcome. If we can force these, the rest of the door should open just fine."

"That's still a metal bar the size of your thumb. How do you propose we force them?"

"Why do you think I carry this thing?" she said, shrugging off the wrench from her back.

She hoisted it from the ground and tightened its jaws around the hexagonal hub of the central gear. When it was firmly clamped in place, she unsheathed the cheater bars and screwed them together, inserting one end into a hole in the wrench head and heaving with all of her might.

"Lend a shoulder," she said, refitting it into a hole that angled the bar lower.

The two of them crouched, braced a shoulder against the far end of the bar, and put their backs into it. Slowly the locking bars started to creak. They worked together, counting off and then thrusting against the bar, earning a fraction of a degree of additional rotation each time. Before long the Coopers returned.

"We didn't see anyone, but we got far enough down to see a light at the other end of the warehouse, so there's probably another guard on the other side. And he probably doesn't have a key either, so he'd have to come through this door. What's going on here?" Lil said.

"Give us a hand, we've just about got this," Gunner grunted.

The four of them working together made steady progress until, with a final heave, the locking bars curled free of the gear and it turned freely, drawing back the braces and unlocking the door.

"Hoo-wee!" Coop said, wiping the sweat from his brow. "Is this what they have the ladies doing down in Caldera? I pictured them teaching you how to be classy and all that."

Nita removed the wrench and looped the ropes through its jaws to hoist it onto her back. "Well, sometimes class can come in handy. But you don't need class if you have a monkey-toe."

"Let's go!" Lil said, shoving the door open.

"Take it slow," Gunner said. "I've heard bad things about the sort of stuff they've got in here. And we don't know if it is empty."

They stepped inside and pushed the door shut. Nita turned the flame in her lamp to full, and each of the others pulled strange glass and brass cylindrical contraptions from their equipment and twisted the ends. The ubiquitous green light blossomed inside the devices, revealing their surroundings. Though the light didn't cut far into the darkness, it was clear the building was massive and cavernous. There were no walls inside, only huge shelves reaching dozens of feet into the air, nearly to the ceiling. The warehouse was easily large enough to contain several whole buildings from some of the less industrial portions of the city.

The entryway was caged off within the building, a small chamber set apart from the main warehouse. A desk protected by bars sat to one side, no doubt meant to be manned by a clerk charged with auditing what came in and went out during operation. The gate leading to the rest of the warehouse wasn't nearly as sturdy as the one outside, but it had enough piping and tubing running around its edge to pique Nita's curiosity. As Coop and Lil investigated the gate, Nita held her lamp close and followed the tubes.

"This one's pretty rickety, and the walls and the fug should make sure no one can hear if we bang around a bit. I bet Gunner and I can force it without your fancy doodad," Coop said.

"Let's do it. Every time a patrol goes overhead there's a chance they will notice the guard is down."

Nita let them go to work heaving at the door while she continued to trace out the tubes. One led to a valve lever on the clerk desk. From there it led up over the door to a lever that hung down below the edge, and then over the cage. She raised her lamp higher.

"Stop forcing the door!" she yelped, when she spotted its final destination.

The rest of the crew looked first to her widened eyes, then to what they were locked upon. It was an array of what looked remarkably like firearms. They were mounted above the cage and pointed downward, and in place of their trigger assemblies were a series of pneumatic plungers.

"If you force the door open it will open the valve and fire them," Nita said.

"You sure?" Coop asked.

"No, but do you want to test it?"

"I reckon not. So what do we do about it?"

She pulled a pair of locking pliers from her tool sash. "Give me a boost."

Gunner laced his fingers together, and she planted a boot in his hands, stepping up until she was level with the top of the cage. She adjusted the pliers and reached through the bars to clamp them down good and hard on the tube leading to the triggers.

"Okay," she said, hopping down. "That should do it. But just in case, let's make this quick. All at once."

They braced themselves, each casting a wary glance above, then on the count of three charged the gate. Under their combined force the door crashed open, flipping the trigger lever. The group tumbled in a heap down the short flight of stairs leading down to the factory floor. Behind them, they heard the slow whistle of pressure slipping through her improvised clamp.

"Oh no," Nita blurted. She leapt to her feet and scrambled up the stairs, then up the outside of the cage. With a panicked swat she flipped the trigger lever back down and retreated back to the floor. The whistle faded away, and the guns remained mercifully silent. She breathed a sigh of relief and climbed up to retrieve her pliers.

"Can we get to looting now?" Lil asked, evidently unfazed by the rapid-fire near catastrophes. "So far this heist has been mostly opening doors."

"Yes, go. Just don't get killed," Gunner said. "We need all of us alive and carrying as much as we can to make this job worth our while. Lil and Coop, you'll be after anything that looks like it is worth a bundle. Nita, since you have an eye for it, you'll be after technology, information, and medicine. I'll go for weaponry."

"Big surprise there. Come on, Brother. I'm itching to go shopping!" Lil said.

They spread out, Lil and Coop scampering like schoolchildren while Gunner and Nita moved with more care and purpose. As mazelike as this place seemed to be, it *was* a warehouse. The fug folk had no intention of hiding anything, no doubt making the reasonable assumption that the toxic atmosphere, the network of spies, the patrol ships, the guards, and the traps would be enough to keep potential thieves from making it this far. Aisles were clearly marked, and there were even inventory booklets at the end of each row listing the contents and their locations. Nita rushed from booklet to booklet.

"Medical: Equipment," she read aloud. "Medical: Documentation. Medical: Drugs!"

She sprinted down the aisle. Leading from the floor to the top of the shelves was a rolling ladder on a runner, the likes of which one might find in a large library. Nita took a running leap and grabbed onto the ladder, coasting along with it as rows of oddly named canisters whisked by her. Finally she grasped the edge of a shelf and brought herself to a stop.

"Tomocin," she said with a hushed voice.

It was a small, unassuming jar with a spring top, the kind you might store preserves in, and yet everything she had done in the last few days had been to get her hands on it. The jar was filled to the brim with a fine white powder. At a glance she might have mistaken it for sugar. She carefully stowed three jars of the precious stuff, then began to load up on other jars with useful indications. When she'd filled a sack, she slid down the ladder and rushed back to the edge of the aisle to find her way to the books that would teach her how to administer the treatments.

The minutes rolled by as she weighed herself down with medicines, design books, and gadgets. At first she took her time to find things that were sturdy enough to survive rough handling and still fetch a high price. There were clocks, strange tools, complex locks, and items that, even with a description, she couldn't comprehend. Gradually she used less and less care, choosing instead to get her bags filled as quickly as possible. Every passing moment filled her with more anxiety, since what little planning they had done was focused on escaping before they were noticed, and there was little hope of that happening if they didn't get moving quickly. As she progressed down the aisle devoted to the more technical devices, they steadily grew in size and complexity, tools being replaced with machinery, then replacement parts, and finally something that managed to force all of the fear and worry from her mind, allowing her inner engineer to practically froth at the mouth.

#

Elsewhere in the warehouse, Gunner and the Coopers crossed paths. Unlike Nita, they had been focusing on quantity over quality from the beginning. Gunner was a walking armory now, strapped with rifles, pistols, ammunition, and strange assemblages of metal pipes, wooden stocks, and triggers that seemed far too large to be a weapon intended to be fired by or at a human. The siblings had grabbed anything and everything light enough to carry and small enough to shove in a sack.

"What's that big brass tube there, Gunner?" Lil asked breathlessly.

"Something called a 'rocket-propelled grenade.' I am thoroughly interested in two of those three terms, so I suspect I'll find it quite useful," he said.

"I got a mess of booze and some of those tins of fancy fish eggs they charge so much for. Plus, I got a couple of those cameras and the stuff to take a *pile* of pictures. I reckon we could start taking our own girlie pictures. They always sell real good."

"Yeah, but where you gonna get the girlies?" Lil asked.

"Well, there's you, and there's Nita, and Butch."

"If you think me or Nita are gonna dress up like them girlies you're always selling pictures of, that brain of yours needs adjusting. And no offense to Butch, but she don't seem like her pictures would fetch much of a price."

"Well, what did *you* get?"

"Perfume and a bunch of bolts of that fancy fabric they make down here, and some of them good binoculars and telescopes and such," she said. "I still got some sacks left. I want to do another round to fill 'em up."

"Coop, Gunner, Lil!" Nita called out as loud as she dared.

"There you are," Lil said. "Where's your sacks? Time's a-wasting!"

"How much can the *Wind Breaker* carry?" she asked.

"More than we can, so get to filling those sacks."

"No, I mean it. How much can it carry?"

"We ain't been able to overload it yet. When the cap'n had the fuggers fix it up for the long-haul trips, he had them swap out the envelope for one of them heavy-lifter ones they use for hauling coal up from the mines down here."

"Could it handle three tons?"

All eyes turned to Gunner.

"Just about. The handling would suffer, but it would get off the ground. Why?"

"Follow me. Bring the sacks. I think I've found a way to really make the most of this," she said.

She led the way to a loading area, which contained all sorts of large steam engines ready for installation, and where an enormous and curious device—a long, flat platform on wide, rubber-studded wheels—stuttered and hissed. The platform's bed was already loaded with a few miniature boilers and small steam engines, the likes of which only the fug folk seemed able to create. An arm's-worth of sacks had already been loaded onto it and were well secured. On one side of the platform was a glowing firebox hooked up to the most complicated tangle of pipes, tubes, gears, springs, levers, and valves any of the crewmembers had ever seen. A seat was bolted to the side of the mechanism and surrounded by wheels and levers.

"What the hell is that?"

"They just call it a 'steam hauler.' It is a steam-powered wagon. All we need to do is get the goods out here so they can be loaded, right? This can haul five times as much as we can. We load it up, roll it out, and empty it into the gig."

"Can you operate it?" Gunner asked.

"I think I can get it moving."

"Let's do it then. Get this thing loaded up."

Coop turned his head, angling his ear toward the wall. "Uh-oh. You folks hear that?"

"What is it?"

"I think we been found out. I'm hearing turbines and a lot of yelling."

"Let's just get out of here!" Lil said. "Take what we got. It's already worth more than we made in the last few years put together."

"No. I've got a better idea. Coop, get to the door, clear it of fug folk, and do what it takes to block it, then get back here and start loading this bed with anything you can."

He fired off a salute. "This'll be fun!" he called out while running.

"Nita, you get to loading this up. I want this bed *filled*."

"What should I do?" Lil asked.

"I don't care how, but get yourself up to the roof with the flares. And listen very carefully, because you're not going to have much time to explain this to the captain…"

#

On the *Wind Breaker*, Captain Mack still toyed with his cigar, quietly questioning if taking a few puffs would be worth the potentially fatal breaths of fug that would come along with them. Butch was watching the darkness in the direction of the warehouse, while Wink took advantage of the patrolman's unconscious state to illustrate precisely how he felt about the fug folk in general, and this one in particular. He may not have had words, but he was quite expressive with bodily functions.

"Good to know where your loyalties lie, Wink," Captain Mack said. He looked toward the center of Fugtown. A pair of faint glows signaled the return of their "rescuers." "They are taking their sweet time of it. Just about time to haul up the anchor, I'd say. And to get this fella out of sight."

He shoved the sleeping and lightly soiled patrolman with his boot, sending him tumbling through a hatch and into the ship. With him safely out of sight, he took the controls and began massaging the levers. In a maneuver that had taken several years to master, he managed to dislodge the anchor from the ground with nothing more than some fancy winch work and an engine-assisted swing of the gondola. The groaning anchor winch was still rumbling inside the ship when Butch pointed and bellowed something. He turned to see the sky light up with an orange-green flare that drifted slowly downward. Instantly the approaching ships' engines roared as they shifted toward the warehouse.

"Figures my crew would have the worst possible timing."

He pushed his own engines to the limit, nodding in appreciation as the repairs Nita had made didn't blast to bits under the strain. The *Wind Breaker* surged forward, but it became clear quite quickly that the fug folk saved the best ships for themselves. Captain Mack's craft was never known for its speed. Its turbines were selected for good maneuvering and long journeys. Even the tow ship was gaining on them. Fortunately, the *Wind Breaker* was much closer to the warehouse… but not nearly as close as the patrol ship that was now becoming visible directly below the flare. He glanced back at the other ships. At this rate they would reach the warehouse at the same time he did, leaving the *Wind Breaker* outnumbered three ships to one.

"Figures…" he repeated.

Chapter 14

"Okay, boys and girls!" Lil cried out in combined exhilaration and fear. "I think we got their attention!"

She huddled behind the stout masonry of the warehouse's roof access. It was a brick enclosure that sheltered a staircase leading down into the building from the roof, or at least it had been a few minutes ago. Now it was rapidly being reduced to rubble by a hail of fléchettes launched from the twin guns of the hovering patrol ship.

"We just need a few more seconds!" Nita called from inside.

"Well, I don't know if you're gonna get it," she replied. A brief lull in gunfire gave her a chance to lean out and unload a few rounds with her stolen rifle. Like most things they'd found since they'd approached the warehouse, it was an order of magnitude better made than what they'd been using. The weapon barked a short sharp report and actually managed to buckle the metal mounting of one of the fléchette guns. "I hope I live long enough to get good with this thing."

The sound of a second and much more familiar set of turbines drew the attention of Lil and the patrol ship alike. The senior officer of the patrol ship pulled out his megaphone. "Attention unknown ship. You will leave this area immediately, or you *will* be fired on. We are in the process of eliminating a trespasser and will not be interfered with."

"I don't rightly care," came the captain's bellowed reply.

"The cap'n's here! You ready yet!" Lil cried.

"We're ready!" Nita called back.

"Finally! Cap'n! Down here!" Lil waved. A fresh round of fléchettes from the intact deck gun sent her back under cover. "Hang on, I'll light up another flare so's you can see me!"

She strapped her rifle to her back and pulled out the second flare, little more than a bundle of brightly burning material strapped to a small parachute. Lighting the fuse and hefting it once, she made ready to heave it straight up, but a thought struck her. With a shrug, she hurled it instead directly at the deck of the patrol ship, which had pulled quite close in its attempts to perforate her. The flare sparked to brilliant life just as it landed on the deck, causing a few moments of panic as they tried to figure out what she had thrown. It didn't last long, but it lasted long enough for the *Wind Breaker* to get close enough to make it clear to the patroller that it had no intention of avoiding a collision. The ship hastily withdrew, and the *Wind Breaker* roared overhead, unfurling its rope ladder as it went. Lil, with her typical disregard for safety and common sense, dove off the roof after the rope and just barely snagged it, hauling herself quickly inside.

There she found Butch, holding tight to the railing around the hatch after having sent down the ladder. Lil ran to the speaking tube in the gig room and hollered into it.

"Cap'n, I'm gonna start unhooking the gig." Since the winch for the gig was the strongest and the hatch above the gig was one of the largest, they frequently detached the gig to haul in larger cargo. To facilitate this, the final length of chain connected to the gig was fastened in place with removable bolts, above which were heavy-duty hooks. Lil deployed a pair of wrenches and began loosening the bolts. "When you see the rest of the crew, chase them down and we'll pick them up."

"That's going to be a mite difficult, seeing as how I don't know where they are, and, without a distraction, these patrol ships on either side of me aren't going to give me the time to find them," he replied.

"I don't think you'll have to worry about that. Just get the ship moving down that there street, and don't stop for nothing."

At that moment a deafening crack of thunder split the air from below as a large section of the warehouse wall exploded outward. The enemy ships pulled back, their crew shouting and scanning the area for artillery. Shattered bits of masonry were still raining down to the ground when a wheel-squealing, piston-pumping contraption came roaring through the hole in the wall. It was the steam cart, mounded with all manner of stolen goods. Nita sat at the controls on the front end, her goggles firmly in place. She was wrestling to keep the vehicle from plowing into the buildings on either side of the street while the rest of the crew clung desperately to the mound of loot. It rattled along the road at a speed that clearly came as a surprise to its passengers. A brilliant beam of light projected from a curved reflector above the over-stoked firebox, lighting up the street ahead of them.

"What the hell is that?" the captain hollered over the speaking tube.

"That's our haul. Pretty good one, huh?" Lil said. "Get us over it."

"We're not going to have any luck loading that thing up with these three ships all over us," the captain said. The sounds of fléchettes digging into the wood of the gondola were already coming in bursts. "If you're going to drop the gig, do it on my mark."

"Aye, Cap'n."

The *Wind Breaker* pitched upward, phlogiston pumping into its envelope and its altitude rising. One of the patrol ships flew beside them, its lone functioning gun focused on the madly weaving steam cart below. The other patrol ship was behind them but gaining fast, peppering them with fléchettes that had so far been unable to puncture the additional patches they'd applied during their days of preparation. The art of ship-to-ship combat was effectively reduced to achieving and holding the high ground. Whichever ship was highest had the best shot at the envelopes of the others while simultaneously protecting its own. Captain Mack had made certain his cannons were loaded, but without his full crew they would be slow to reload, so he was reluctant to fire them until he was certain he needed to. Though he wasn't precisely certain why his recently rescued deckhand was determined to cut the gig loose, so long as it was going to happen, it may as well serve a purpose.

He eased the ship over one of the two huge fans that gave the patrol ship its speed and slowly descended. "You ready to cut her loose?"

"Just gotta yank the last bolt, Cap'n. Waiting for your mark," Lil yelled over to the speaking tube. She had a pair of pliers clamped onto the final bolt and was holding tight to the railing around the gig hatch as the boat dangled against the one remaining connection.

"Almost… almost… *now*!"

"Launching gig!" Lil pulled the bolt loose and the boat plummeted a short distance before colliding with the port fan of the patrol ship.

The powerful blades easily chewed through the wood of the boat, but not without consequence. Damaged blades buckled and finally tore free, one launching almost straight up and missing the *Wind Breaker* by inches. The patrol ship wasn't so lucky, with one blade biting into the deck of the gondola and another slicing open the top of the envelope to release a blinding flare of fluorescent phlogiston lancing into the sky. It was enough to send the stricken ship spiraling quickly to the ground, its distress whistle blasting all the while.

"Whoo-hoo! That's one down!" Lil crowed. She rushed to the speaking tube. "Listen, Cap'n. We gotta get lower. Gunner and Nita figure the best way to do this is to hook the gig hoist to that cart thing there. After that we can haul the whole thing away."

"Were you planning on consulting with me about this?"

"That's what I'm doing now, Cap'n. You reckon we can do it?"

There was a brief and potent silence. "I suppose we'll find out."

#

"Ha *ha*! That's one down!" Gunner echoed from below, watching as the patrol ship collided with a row of empty buildings. The cart veered, nearly knocking him off. "Perhaps you should slow this thing just a touch, so that they can lower down the winch chains."

"Slow it down…" Nita said, glancing at the dizzying array of controls. "I think this one might do that."

She pulled a lever that instead gave such a surge of acceleration the front wheels nearly left the ground.

"I said *slower*!"

"I don't know *how* to make it slower," she said, hastily resetting the lever and at least bringing them back down to their original speed.

"But you insisted on reading through that manual."

"Yes, to learn how to *start* it. Stopping it is another matter entirely."

A row of fléchettes whistled through the air, tracing a line across the road and sweeping toward the cart. Nita pulled hard on the stick she'd been able to determine was responsible for steering. The cart skittered across the cobblestones, fishtailing slightly before straightening again.

"Not so sharp on the turns," Gunner cried, holding tight to one of the ropes lashed over the pile of goods to keep them in place.

"Look, do *you* want to drive?" she snapped, veering again to avoid another string of fléchettes.

"Just don't kill us before the patrol does!" he said. Still clutching the rope for stability, he reached into his jacket, drew a long-barreled pistol, and tried to level it at the second patrol ship, which was firing one gun at them and the other at the *Wind Breaker*.

The patrol ship maneuvered nearly on top of the *Wind Breaker*, its shots striking the envelope with enough force to stick in but not yet puncture it. He squeezed off a shot, failing to hit anything vital but certainly giving the crew something to think about.

"Here come the chains! Keep 'er steady, Nita!" Coop said.

"I'm not making any promises!" Nita said.

The chains reeled out more and more, then suddenly stopped, having reached their limit with a dozen feet to go. Nita eyed the looming buildings on each side of the street. The city obviously wasn't designed to have an airship touching down in its avenues. From rooftop to rooftop there was room enough for the gondola to fit, but with mere feet to spare on either side. To get close enough, the ship was going to have to thread a needle at top speed while being shot at. It was something a sober, thoughtful man would never attempt. Captain Mack, on the other hand, eased the nose of the ship right in.

"Almost!" Coop said, reaching out for the swinging chain as the gondola scraped off window boxes and tore free flagpoles from the fronts of houses. The first of four hooks was just inches from Coop's fingers now, but he couldn't reach it without letting go of the strap he'd been using to brace himself. Being Coop, the solution was simple enough. He let go. "I got it! Uh-oh…"

He barely managed to get his fingers firmly around the hook when Mack had to pull the ship upward to avoid a balcony. The motion pulled the chains five feet into the air, and Coop right along with them.

"Coop, you idiot!" Gunner growled, scrambling over the mound of loot and reaching for his dangling crewmate's foot. "Nita, bring us *gently* to the right!"

"I ain't so worried about gentle so much as *fast*!" Coop countered, his voice a bit more steady than it ought to be for a man racing over the street hanging from an airship.

Nita feathered the control stick and managed to move the cart in range of the steadily lowering Coop without dislodging Gunner. When the deckhand had been successfully hauled aboard again, the pair guided the hook down and looped it around the support above one of the wheels. The *Wind Breaker* loomed over them, inching the other chains into reach.

"Boys, could you hurry it up?" Nita said, nerves fluttering her voice.

"Doing the best we can," Coop said.

"Well, do it faster! We've got two problems! We're running out of road!" she said.

"How can you see that in this soup?" Gunner asked, struggling to secure the second hook.

"That's the other problem."

Ahead, the street that had thus far been mercifully straight approached a T-junction that would put their forward progress to a sudden and catastrophic end. Illuminating that hazard was a pair of additional patrol ships answering the distress whistle of the one they had blown out of the sky. The distant ships focused primarily on the airship, though at their extreme distance the fléchettes scattered in an unpredictable cloud of razor-sharp darts. They clanged off the cart's hefty boiler, punctured pipes, and whistled by the exposed crew.

"Almost got it," Coop said, straining against the final chain to get enough slack to hook it in place.

"Hey! You all stop messing around down there! Cap'n says you've got to the count of ten before he pulls up! And he's up to five already. Four. Three. Two..."

"Just... a touch... more..." Coop groaned.

"Time's up!" she yelled.

The ship jerked upward, punching the hook through the side of the platform rather than hooking under it.

"That'll do her, I guess," Coop said, scratching his head.

The chains groaned against their load, but for a few moments the cart continued to trundle along the ground.

"The *Wind Breaker can* lift this thing, can't it?" Nita said, eyes widening as the details of the approaching wall of buildings became more distinct.

"It can lift us," Gunner assured her. "It can lift us." Upon repeating, it sounded strangely like he was trying to convince himself.

Finally the wheels began to stutter and skip on the ground, then the whole cart was hoisted into the air. As it rose, it rotated, crashing through hanging store signs and wooden shutters. Nita, Gunner, and Coop watched silently as they drew closer to the end of the street, each mentally comparing their rate of ascension to the remaining distance and not liking the results of the equation. Worse, the closer they came to the patrol ships, the more on target their weapon fire was.

"We're not going to clear the buildings… We're not going to clear the buildings!" Nita cried.

"Maybe we'll get lucky and they'll kill us with them darts before we hit the wall," Cooper offered.

"You all need to hold on and cover your ears. We're just about lined up!" Lil called down from above.

Nita salvaged just enough of her panicked brain to obey, wrapping an arm around one of the winch chains and plugging her ears. She watched through squinted eyes and dusty goggles, the buildings and patrol ships nearly on top of them. Then came the sound, a roaring blast that made the detonation of the warehouse wall sound like a whisper in comparison. Captain Mack had fired both sets of forward cannons simultaneously. Their scattershot load tore effortlessly through the envelopes of the enemy ships, one with a direct hit that caused the gondola to plummet a short distance to the vacant houses below, releasing its load of phlogiston in one glorious green plume of light. The other strike was a glancing one, yet it pulverized the propeller on one side to send the ship in a slower but more erratic path.

The kick from firing the cannons cut the ship's forward speed drastically, causing the dangling load of crew and loot to swing forward. Nita, Gunner, and Coop hung on for dear life, time seeming to slow to a crawl as their suspended cart lurched forward and strained at its chains. Though the slowing effect of the cannons was enough for the ship and the payload to clear the roof, they didn't do so cleanly. The cart bashed like a wrecking ball through a stout chimney, dusting the crew with shattered masonry and nearly knocking them loose.

"Is that it? Was that all of them?" Coop asked, shaking his head. "I hope so. If anything else sets us to spinning I'm going to end up making an offering."

Nita scanned around them as the winches began to draw them closer to the ship.

"It looks like there's two left," she said.

The air split again with another cannon blast, this time to their rear. It knocked the pursuing patrol ship from the sky and sent the cart on another pendulous swing.

"Make that one," she corrected, holding tight.

They turned to the final pursuer. The craft could easily have been the *Wind Breaker*'s sister ship. Its overall shape was the same, and it had a similar—though considerably bulkier—turbine configuration. Notably absent was anything resembling armaments. In place were large grappling cannons on either side of the deck.

Coop looked. “Aw, that's just a tow ship. What could that thing do?”

As an answer, a thump echoed as a grappler was launched in their direction. It traveled in a low arc, crashing down on the aft railing and beginning to reel in.

“What have I told you about tempting fate?” Gunner growled, slapping Coop on the back of the head.

Captain Mack pushed the engines hard, tearing the ship free of the tow ship's grip at the cost of most of the rear railing.

“Now would be a good time to get in here,” Lil called from above as the cart drew in as far as the winch would bring it. The crew scrambled up through the gig hatch. “Cap'n says Wink is hopping up and down something fierce. I think we've got something worse than a tow ship on the way.”

Chapter 15

The *Wind Breaker* breeched through the surface of the fug at full speed, dragging lavender streamers behind. Their mission in the fug had taken them far from the city center of Keystone, but not so far that the local mountaintops weren't speckled with homes, workshops, and lantern-topped mooring posts. Night had fallen while they were below, but families sitting down at the dinner table were treated to quite a show as Captain Mack turned his prow toward the mountains while the tow ship burst from beneath them.

"Is that cart of yours secure? If we lose that loot, we're through," he barked into the speaking tube.

"I'm on it, Cap'n," Coop replied.

"Gunner and Nita, I want you on deck. Lil, reload all cannons."

The crew stowed their masks in the gig room equipment chest and jumped to their tasks. Gunner climbed out onto the deck first, Nita close behind. It had not fared well. Lines of fléchettes crisscrossed the deck, splintering struts, severing ropes, and turning the envelope into a veritable pincushion. The gummy layer of self-sealant and a few strategically placed reinforcement patches had kept it reasonably intact despite the assault, but even so a few leaks still faintly fluoresced from the residual fug.

"Nita, I'm hearing some steam escaping, and the second starboard turbine is feeling sluggish. Get on that," Captain Mack ordered.

Nita nodded, looking to Mack.

"Oh my gosh! Captain, are you all right?!"

The captain had not fared much better than his ship. A long, bloody wound ran across his left side, presumably where a fléchette had brushed him, and a crooked metal dart stuck out of this thigh. Butch was already by his side on one knee, applying a bandage while the captain continued to guide the ship. Wink cowered at his healthy leg.

"It was a ricochet. It's nothing. Get on the repairs!"

She lingered for a moment more but forced her concern aside and scanned the darkness for venting steam.

"Gunner, I don't want another grappling hook taking any more of my ship. Get that tow ship off our back. I think it's time we broke out a 'telescope.'"

"With pleasure," Gunner said, running to the railing and pulling free one of the blankets concealing an installed and operational fléchette gun salvaged from the wailer.

"I'll swing around. Make quick work of it," the captain ordered.

The engines labored and the ship slowly came around. Gunner's eyes gleamed as he leveled the weapon at the moonlit tow ship. "Let's see what this can do."

He pulled the trigger and sent a string of stolen darts at the enemy. They swiftly disappeared into the night, none seeming to have hit the target.

"A bit difficult to aim at night," he said, furrowing his brow. He adjusted and fired again, this time receiving the reward of a distant patter of impacts. Another string punched a large enough hole in their pursuer's envelope to prevent it from maintaining altitude, and it disappeared back into the fug, where the escaping gas lit up the cloud like green lightning.

"Good work, Gunner," the captain said. "How's the repair coming, Ms. Graus?"

"Won't be a moment. It was just a pipe puncture," she said, clamping a cuff onto a pipe. "I'll do a more permanent repair when I can."

"Okay," Coop yelled from the hatch. "Loot's all hooked up. You folks know there's a sleeping fugger down here?"

"Ignore him. Just get up here and keep your eyes peeled. Wink still seems a bit concerned."

He climbed up, a look of disappointment on his face. "You mean you already took out the tow ship?"

"Indeed. The new gun worked like a charm!" Gunner said like a proud father.

Coop tipped his head and furrowed his brow in the effort of thought. "How many fuggers you figure we killed?"

"Aw, I wouldn't be surprised if we didn't kill any. The nice thing about these ships is they tend to crash pretty slow. And them fuggers are tough," the captain said, wincing as Butch yanked free the dart in his leg without warning.

Coop sighed. "That was pretty easy, when you really think about it."

Gunner scowled. "Didn't we *just* have that chat about tempting fate?"

"What else could they throw at us?"

Wink, who seldom made a sound besides his incessant tapping, audibly squealed. He hopped desperately for the hatch below decks until he reached the end of his harness leash and was jerked from his feet. A few moments later, the sound that his sensitive ears had picked up became audible to the others. It sounded like propellers, the sort that might be on a patrol ship, but wrong somehow. The sound was deeper and less distinct. Then came the motion. A section of the fug began to bulge upward, like a bubble forming on the surface of a tar pit. A vigorous churning appeared around nearly half the dome, at least a dozen propellers chopping at the surface of the fug. The purple mist slid away from the top of the bulge, revealing first several strings of serrated fins, then the gleaming sheen of some sort of metallic cloth.

Two brilliant shafts of light suddenly erupted from beneath the fug, spotlights of some kind, burning like lime lights. They pivoted and swept as the thing continued to rise. It was an airship, but larger than anything they'd encountered before. When it finally cleared the fug, it was revealed to have three envelopes keeping it aloft. The main one was an armored and barbed mountain of a sack, easily five times the size of the whole of the *Wind Breaker*. The secondary balloons were a bit less than half the size of the main one, slung behind the main one to support what was less a ship and more a multitier gun platform. Cannons and lesser guns utterly ringed the platform, and manned turrets even spanned along the front edge of the envelope, while droning fans lined the entire rear half of the main envelope's circumference. It was a vicious and predatory thing, a warship without question.

"Ho-lee hell… a dreadnought…" Coop said, his jaw dropping open.

"Gunner, slap Coop for me, would you?" the captain said.

Gunner obliged, delivering a motivating slap to the back of his crewmate's head. "Your talking privileges are revoked."

"Have you ever seen anything like this before?" Nita asked once she'd wrestled aside enough fear to speak.

"Withholding repairs is how the fuggers keep ships in line. Withholding resources is how they keep cities in line. The dreadnought is how they keep nations in line. Just knowing the thing exists has been enough to keep both Circa and Westrim from forming an army and breaking their hold on us," he explained, shutting down the turbines and turning a knob that shut off the lights. "We must have got our hands on something really good, if they sent that thing after us."

"Why did you shut off the turbines? Shouldn't we escape?"

"It is faster than us, and there's nothing we have that will be able to knock it out before it can knock us out. Best we can do is run silent and hope it looks the wrong way, then run."

They all stood in silence, watching the spotlights at the forward edge of the dreadnought methodically scan for the *Wind Breaker*. As it did, the captain spoke orders just loudly enough to be heard.

"Gunner, how are we on ammunition for the dart gun?"

"Not much left, Captain. We only had what was left in the wailer, and what we could salvage from what had been fired at us."

"Make sure it is ready to fire. If you've got anything in that collection of yours that might do some good, be ready to use it. Coop, help him haul up whatever he thinks he can use. Glinda, you'd best load up on fresh bandages." They quickly got to work. "Ms. Graus, how is that repair?"

"Strong enough."

"Strong enough to take a little more pressure than perhaps your new boiler was really meant for?"

"For a little while, probably."

He was silent for a time, the two of them alone on the deck.

"You done good work for us in these last few days, Nita," he said. "It takes a special sort to find a place on a ship like this. You ain't perfect, but I think there'd be a place for you."

She sensed that, for this moment, he wasn't speaking as a superior officer addressing his crew. He was McCulloch West, the man, wishing to share something that he might not get a chance to say in the future.

"I never would have set foot on a ship like this if I didn't have to… but I must admit that I feel I've lived more in these last few days than in the years before," she said.

He nodded. "A ship may cut your days short, but it'll make sure the ones you've got are filled to the brim. I call it a fair trade." He squinted his eyes, and his face hardened. When he spoke, it was once again with the tone of authority. "That spotlight is coming our way. We're made. Go find Lil and help her feed the firebox. A double load of coal. No slow-burn. I want us running hot, Ms. Graus. Too hot."

By the time he finished delivering the order, a spotlight cast its blinding light upon them. He pushed the turbines to life. Nita dashed for the hatch and navigated the halls of the ship. Lil waited near the aft magazine.

"Come on, we need to feed the firebox. A double load," Nita said.

"He wants to overstoke? Must be something real bad out there, huh?" Lil said, running quickly toward the fuel room.

"A dreadnought."

She shot Nita a look that seemed wholly out of place. It was fear. "The dreadnought. I never seen it. I was always kind of glad about that."

"What is this overstoking?" Nita asked.

They reached the fuel room and began to load up. "It was something he used to tell us about. He got in a real bad scrape on his first ship, years ago. The *Vanguard* or something like that. A dozen wailers. He overstoked the boiler to squeeze some extra speed out."

"Did it work?"

"Well, he's alive, but he ain't got that ship no more, so yes and no."

They made their way to the boiler and began to feed in the coal. There was a distant thump, then the ship rocked violently to the side. The captain's voice came blaring out of the speaking tube.

"We are taking fire. Get that box stoked. Lil, you'll be on both fore and aft cannons. Keep them loaded. Grapeshot aft, standard shot fore. Nita, on deck. I want you on hand for repairs. I'm going to need everything this ship can give me. I can't afford to be coping with disabled controls, or we're through."

They finished their current task and Nita rushed for the deck. The ship lurched aside again, not with the suddenness of a weapon hit but with the swing of a dodge. She climbed to the deck to find the dreadnought already nearly on top of them. Captain Mack pushed his ship to climb, but their heavy load robbed them of their nimbleness. The dreadnought, for its size, was terrifying in its maneuverability. The one thing it didn't seem to be able to do was climb quickly, so the battle was, for the moment, a slow race skyward. Mack had been able to keep them just barely above the main cannons. The attack ship did not appear to be fully manned, leaving several of the upper turrets without operators, but at least two were harrying them with darts that made those of the patrollers and the wailers look like toothpicks.

"They aren't aiming for the envelope, and they weren't targeting direct hits when we were in range of the main cannons. They must be trying to recover the cargo intact. The higher we go, the less likely they are to be willing to shoot us down," the captain said as Gunner heaved a sack of weaponry onto the deck. "Gunner, I want those lights out. Those fuggers can see well enough in the dark, we don't need them getting any help. Once those are out, fire at will. Now's not the time to hold anything back."

"On it, Captain," Gunner said. He rushed to the fléchette gun and pitched it down toward the spotlights.

The brilliance of the light made it difficult to target directly, but a few quick crisscrosses of the approximate area managed to shatter the glass of the first light and fracture its workings. While targeting the second one, the fléchette gun ran dry of ammo.

"Give me the grinder," Gunner said. Coop tugged free a weapon made from a ring of gun barrels attached to a box with a crank on one side and a belt of ammunition on the other. The bottom side had a wide clamp, which he heaved onto the railing and tightened up before tilting the contraption in the general direction of the light and turning the handle. With a sound like a row of soldiers firing off their rifles at once, the weapon slung a stream of bullets at their enemy. Barely a dozen shots before it reached the end of its ammo belt, the second light fizzled and died.

Without their lights, the accuracy of the smaller guns suffered, though that was not entirely in the *Wind Breaker*'s favor. Their focus on disabling the ship rather than destroying it suffered as well, and more than a few darts chewed into the envelope. There was no rupture, but a thin stream of gas escaped from a handful of holes too large to be patched by their improvised self-sealing system. At least one inner section of the envelope was compromised.

"Okay, we're going to run for it," Mack said, angling the ship out over the mountains now far below them. "Let's see just how tough their ship really is."

The *Wind Breaker* roared as her rear cannon fired. At this range there was no missing the massive attacker, but despite the direct hit on the envelope, little evidence of any damage, beyond a barely visible plume of green gas at first, appeared. Then it became clear that the dreadnought, though still rising in pursuit, wasn't rising as quickly. They were slowly but steadily gaining a height advantage. After a minute they were well above the top of the enemy and still rising. Perhaps sensing that their quarry was on the verge of being out of range, the gunners intensified their attacks. A flurry of darts thumped against the belly and side of the ship, with a stray shot whizzing past and lodging itself in the harness of one of the pumps under the envelope. It began to vent gas freely, and The *Wind Breaker* swiftly started to descend.

"Ms. Graus, the starboard lift pump is hit. That thing is hooked to all of the envelope chambers. I need you to cut off the flow, or we're going to fall right into the jaws of that monster."

Nita looked up to the malfunctioning machinery, swallowed hard, and took to the rigging.

Captain Mack swung the ship around. "As long as we're tipping down, might as well let them have it with both barrels. Stand by, all crew. Big jolt coming."

She had just reached the broken pump when the order came. It left her with barely the time to hold on tight to the rigging before the guns fired, forcing the already forward-pitched ship to tilt drastically. Anything not tied down, including the crew, tumbled forward. Nita was almost shaken free but managed to keep her grip. She looked down and saw two new green plumes coming from the dreadnought but still no sign that it was on the verge of destruction. Shaking her head, she tried to focus on her work. On the deck of the ship, dealing with the pump would have been a simple task. There were a few manual valves that needed to be closed. Here in the rigging of a ship at battle, it seemed impossible. She could only reach three of the five necessary valves. There was no telling how she would close the others, but she would cross that bridge when she came to it.

"It looks like they won't be able to target us as well if we are directly above them! I'm taking us over! If we have to come down, maybe we can tear them up on the way!"

Nita finished the three accessible valves and then eyed the remaining ones. There were no two ways about it. She'd never be able to reach them from the rigging. Without a second thought she climbed out onto the broken pump itself, which dangled from its mounting braces and coughed at the gas it was venting. She moved hand over hand until she could reach the valves, then swung her legs up to hook a brace. She reached out with a wrench and made short work of the fourth valve, then got busy on the last.

As she gave it a final turn, she heard a thump from below that was different from the rest, followed by the worrying crunch of wood. The dreadnought had launched ropes tipped with barbed harpoons directly up from the main deck, between the main envelope and the first small one. They bit into the belly of the ship near the stern and yanked downward, swinging the ship forward. Nita's precarious grip slipped, and she tumbled down to the deck, striking the planks painfully and sliding toward the rear of the ship as the angle became ever more extreme. She picked up speed, knocking free lines of fléchettes, and her eyes briefly met with those of Coop and Gunner as she skated past them. Then, suddenly, there was no deck beneath her.

Again time slowed. She had slipped off the back of the gondola, past where the missing railing should have been. Now she was falling toward the dreadnought below, flipping end over end. Darts whizzed past her. With an odd, resonant thud she smacked into the main envelope with enough force to knock the wind from her lungs. It sent her back into the air, striking it again where its slope was steeper. Now she was skidding directly toward one of the slicing propellers. She flipped over, fingers grasping madly for something to hold onto. Finally she found a support rope leading down from the top of the envelope. She was moving too fast to get a firm grip, but she slowed herself enough to avoid being launched into the blades of the propeller when she ran out of envelope. Instead she was dumped into the rigging and thrown violently from strut to rope to chain, then finally down to the deck below.

She coughed and fought to regain her breath, her mind not yet recovered enough to appreciate the miracle of falling from one airship and landing on another. She swept the deck around her with blurred vision. Either because of its hasty need to launch, or simply by design, the ship operated on a skeleton crew. Each fug person rushed to follow orders bellowed through megaphones from a helm near the fore end of the main deck. The crew was so busy they had not yet noticed her.

Reason wormed its way slowly back into her mind. They wanted the stolen cargo back. That was the only reason they hadn't decimated the *Wind Breaker*. Chances were very good they would have no such qualms about killing a stray crewman. If she wanted to survive, even for a few minutes more, she was going to have to get out of sight before they noticed her. And if there was any hope of getting the stolen medicine back to her mother, she was going to have to find some way to help the *Wind Breaker* get away. Stumbling to her feet, she rushed for the nearest hatch to the lower decks.

#

"We lost Nita!" Coop said.

"Is she dead?" Captain Mack asked.

"I don't know. She might have ended up on the dreadnought."

"Then she's dead either way. Looks like she got that leak fixed before she went, but we lost a lot of gas. We're going to have to bleed some altitude, and we can't stay up here or those harpoons will get us. I'm taking us aside."

He guided the rapidly descending *Wind Breaker* to port, swinging down behind the main envelope, then out and away. Gunner scrambled to reach the sack of weapons that had been thrown about the deck by the attacks. It had become lodged in the mounting of one of envelope struts. He fished out a blunderbuss and took aim at one of the propellers as they swept past. Pulling the trigger unleashed a cloud of pellets. At this range the bulk of the blast met its target, causing the motor to vent steam and sputter to a stop. Though there were no fewer than eleven other propellers still functioning, it was heartening to know that the ship wasn't indestructible.

Their drop began to level off as they cleared the side of the craft. The bad news was that this left them at close range and in good position for the dreadnought's deck guns. The good news was that they were now close enough for Coop and Gunner to target the crew with their pistols and rifles. Firing from ship to ship didn't allow any real accuracy, but by maintaining a constant hail of bullets on the way, they managed to keep the enemy gunmen in search of cover. It led to something of a standoff, because they knew that if they attempted to escape, Coop and Gunner wouldn't be able to keep the enemy gunners busy.

"I'm going to slow her up," Captain Mack said.

"I'd advise against it, Captain," Gunner said between shots. "I've only taken out three of their guns and none of their gunmen. If we fall back, the forward guns could fire on you and the helm."

"I don't figure on there being guns there for too much longer," Captain Mack said. He leaned to the speaking tube. "Forward cannons loaded, Lil?"

"Good to go, Cap'n!" came her reply.

He smiled. "Firing starboard cannons."

Firing a shipboard cannon at point blank range is not typically done for quite a few reasons, all of which were perfectly illustrated in the following moments. The blow was devastating, instantly reducing a stretch of the gunship's hull to splinters. Shards of former ship flew in all directions, some pelting those enemy crewmembers lucky enough to be spared the primary blast, much rebounding back and scouring Coop, Gunner, and the captain. The gunship shuddered to one side, the *Wind Breaker* to the other, and then they crashed together, dislodging or damaging most of the guns and leaving the starboard side of Captain Mack's ship badly damaged. The explosion knocked all three crewmembers on the deck to their backs, and there they remained, motionless.

#

Nita was thrown against the wall of an one of the dreadnought's internal hallways as a cloud of splinters left her scraped up and thanking her lucky stars that she'd kept her goggles in place. When the cloud settled down, she saw that the hallway ahead of her was now missing, replaced with rushing wind and moonlight. The damage revealed something else, however. Until now she'd seen precious little of the dreadnought's steam system. Unlike the cheaply and minimally built *Wind Breaker*, the dreadnought was clearly a war machine, meant for battle, and thus meant to withstand attack. The vital workings were hidden deep inside, where even a blast like the one she'd just narrowly avoided could not reach them. In the shattered remnants of the hall, however, the splintered back wall revealed stout steam pipes. She followed what little of them she could see. It wasn't much, but it was enough to give her an idea of where the boiler was. If there was one thing that could destroy this ship in one fell swoop, it was the boiler.

She doubled back and found her way down the stairs, dodging into side halls whenever the rare crewman appeared. A few twists and turns took her into the depths of the ship, where enormous pipes hung in exposed runs along the walls, leading her directly to the boiler. It was massive, as it would have to be in order to get a behemoth like this moving at all, let alone with the speed and agility it had demonstrated. The boiler approached the size of the ones back at home; but just as the ones the fug folk had built for others were unnecessarily complex, that same brilliance had streamlined the workings of this one to be manned by a single fug person standing on an elevated platform at one side of the room like the conductor of an orchestra. He worked like a man possessed, eyes scanning dozens of meters, pulling levers to dump bins of fuel into chutes and twisting valves to regulate pressure.

She climbed onto the catwalk and crept low behind him, though with his level of distraction she could have been beating a bass drum without drawing his attention. It wasn't until she'd slunk two steps away that he finally turned to inspect the sound of her footsteps, and when he did he received a wrench to the side of his head. He crumbled quickly to the ground, and she was left at the controls of the massive ship's power supply. Cranking open some valves and tightening up others, she began dumping extra fuel into the firebox and manipulating the water flow. In essence, she was gathering together the sum total of what she'd learned about how to keep a boiler from blowing—and doing the opposite. One by one, though, safety valves and other fail-safes triggered.

"They *do* know how to build a good boiler when they want to..." she grumbled.

"We are receiving irregular power to the turbines. Get them regulated, now!" came an order from a clearer and much more elaborate version of the *Wind Breaker*'s speaking tube. "Main Engineer, report! ... Report! ... Secondary Engineer, report to the boiler, and bring two guards."

Nita looked around desperately. There wasn't much time left, and it was clear that no amount of standard tinkering was going to get this boiler to explode. She felt around her equipment, searching for something that might do some good. She'd lost a good deal of tools during her fall. Finally her fingers came to rest on an oddly bulging pouch. She pulled it open to find the exposed coil box. As the footsteps of the engineer and his guards began to echo down the hall, an idea came to mind. She leapt down to the floor of the chamber and sprinted to the firebox. Once there she hauled it open, loosened a few screws on the coil box, and threw it inside, slamming the firebox door shut after. She then commenced bashing madly at any connected pipes she could reach.

"Stop right there!" cried a voice a few moments later.

She turned to the doorway to find two guards with weapons raised.

"Go ahead," she replied. "Fire your weapons in the boiler room. Nothing would make me happier."

"That's the Calderan! How did she get on the ship? Best not to kill her. Grab her and bring her to the captain," the engineer said, climbing to the catwalk and beginning to undo her sabotage.

#

On the *Wind Breaker*, the crew had all survived Captain Mack's desperate attack. Butch had made her way back to the deck and was now busy rousing the dazed captain, who'd been knocked back from the controls by the force of the blast. His face was covered in tiny scrapes, and one lens of his glasses was cracked, but he was otherwise intact. He stood and took the controls again.

"On your feet, men. We might still get out of this," he ordered.

The *Wind Breaker*, without him active at the controls, had veered toward the gunship and now butted against it. He tried to steer it away, but dislodged rigging from the larger ship had become entangled with the support belt for his turbines, holding the ships together. He eased the controls in and out, causing the ship to tug away bit by bit, but as he did the remaining crew of the dreadnought wheeled over a pair of strange contraptions.

"Boarding hooks, men! On your feet!" the captain ordered. He reached for his pistols.

"Keep your hands raised. You've got three rifleman targeting you right now."

He turned to find his counterpart on the dreadnought standing on the deck, speaking through a megaphone.

"You really impress me, Captain West," said the enemy captain. "No one has dared to assault anything concealed by the fug in a century. We have kept the dreadnought on standby constantly for decades, but this is the first time under my command that we have had to use it. Again, I applaud you. I'm inclined to believe that it was through little more than an overabundance of raw gall and foolishness that you achieved this, but I doubt that any amount of daring could come so close to success without a keen mind behind it. And no keen mind would place all of its eggs in a single basket. For instance, I am not sure when or how you inserted one of your crew onto my ship, but we've found her."

He signaled and the guards hauled Nita out into view.

"Again, the mere ability to insert her convinces me that you have tricks up your sleeve. In a moment, my men will board your ship. They will search it, and they will recover all that you have stolen. You will also tell us of any information you have been able to deliver to anyone else through whatever means. If you cooperate, you will be allowed to live, and, in time, your fees will be paid and your life will continue. Men, deploy the boarding hooks."

"I really wouldn't do that," Gunner said, his voice slurred from his own brief trip into unconsciousness. He had in his hand what was either a shotgun sawed down to the size of a pistol, or a pistol modified for firing shot. "The last time I fired this, I nearly broke my wrist, but I'm confident that with it I could kill three of you in one shot without aiming."

"I reckon I could take a few myself," Coop said, sitting up and raising his own pistols.

"And I'll mop up what's left," Lil said, emerging from the hatch with her stolen rifle.

"Captain, please. For your own sake and theirs, I beseech you to get your crew under control," the enemy captain said.

"I'd say they are following my standing orders just fine."

"Perhaps your infiltrator can reason with you." He turned to Nita. "Explain to him what you've seen, that nothing he can do can destroy this ship."

He placed the megaphone in front of her mouth. After a steadying breath, she spoke: "Captain Mack. I am not going to plead for my life. I understand that what we do, we do for the ship. But promise me one thing. When this monster goes down, find a way to get the medicine to my mother. And tell her that I'm sorry."

Captain Mack nodded. "We'll do that, Ms. Graus. You can count on it."

"What do you mean by that? Your tampering didn't do *anything* to the boiler," the enemy captain said.

Fate, in one last showing of its fine sense of humor, chose that moment to finish the work Nita had started. The loosened and damaged coil box finally succumbed to the intense heat of the overfed firebox. The nontrith components gave way, allowing the phenomenal amount of power stored in the coiled spring to burst free. A ribbon of nigh indestructible material unfurled in an instant, punching easily through the walls of both the firebox and the water chamber. Its sturdy structure thus compromised, the boiler began to vent superheated steam. Forced upward by the escaping vapor, the whole of the house-sized boiler thrust through the decks, crashing through them as if they were gingerbread and continuing unimpeded through the envelope above. No matter how secure and well-engineered the design, the sack of gas couldn't withstand such massive damage.

The explosion sent the crew flying and threw Nita to the deck along with the captain. The dreadnought continued to splinter and crack, the fore end drooping as the envelope lost the ability to hold it aloft. The secondary envelopes, still intact, held firm to the aft of the ship, and the damaged craft began to come apart. Captain Mack pushed hard at his controls, turning the *Wind Breaker* away from the disintegrating dreadnought. Lil madly scanned the decks of the two halves of the sinking ship. Finally, on the deck of the falling fore end, she saw Nita, clutching a piece of rigging.

"Cap'n! Nita's still down there. We've got to do something," she cried, pointing.

Captain Mack's sharp mind clicked away, his eyes sweeping across his own ship's deck. Finally they came to rest on the cowering and just recently recovered creature at his feet, Wink.

"Give me the longest lifeline we have, and make sure one side is secured," he ordered. He pulled some levers and set the *Wind Breaker* to descending, though the damaged fore end of the dreadnought was moving swiftly away. He plucked up Wink and set him on the control harness. "Do you want to prove your loyalties to me once and for all? To stay on this ship, as a part of this crew?"

Wink gave a very deliberate and very emphatic tap.

Captain Mack took the end of the presented lifeline. He tied a large loop into it, then attached it to Wink's harness. "You see that greenhorn?"

Wink looked to Nita's rapidly retreating form on the deck below. He again tapped.

"Bring her home."

With that, he picked up the creature and hurled him off the edge of the ship.

Wink plummeted to the deflating envelope, where his deft claws quickly found a grip. He looked up, his one eye wild with fear and confusion, then looked down. With a vocal sound that could only have been frustration, the beast scampered down the deflating envelope and into the rigging.

The wind was catching the falling ship now, drawing it under the *Wind Breaker* where no one could see what was happening. Captain Mack guided the ship down and away, doing his best to follow the path of the accelerating descent of the dreadnought. They were close to the surface of the fug, and getting closer. All eyes but the captain's were on the coil of lifeline still on the deck as it whisked foot by foot off the side of the ship. The dreadnought plunged beneath the surface of the fug now, forcing the horrid stuff aside and sending it rushing up on all sides like soil hurled from a crater. Mack restored the levers, slowing the *Wind Breaker* lest they follow the ship into the toxic stuff. They began to climb again, and the lifeline was nearly at its end.

One final loop of line was drawn off the edge and the whole of the rope went taut. They were rising steadily now.

"Start hauling that line in," Mack ordered.

Gunner and Coop jumped to the task, pulling the line up quickly but steadily. Lil looked anxiously over the side as more of the rope was pulled up from the fug. Finally a form became visible. Wink dangled from the line where it had been tied to his harness. A moment later, her arms hooked through the loop but her body motionless, came Nita. They hauled her up to the ship, where Butch rushed to her side. She placed her head on Nita's chest, then hammered at her ribs with two firm blows. It prompted a raking breath, then a deep, hoarse cough from the Calderan girl. She gasped and coughed again, hacking out a wisp of purple vapor.

"Well," she croaked when she looked around to see the crew standing over her. "I always say, there's nothing like a nice vigorous ending to an uneventful day."

Epilogue

A month later, as the setting sun was finally giving way to full night, a small skiff called *The Triumph* waited at Moor Spires. On the deck were two men, Linus and his brother Drew, who were watching to the west.

"There," Drew said, pointing, "They're coming. Right on time, like always. I knew they would."

"I owe you five, then. I'll bet you double or nothing that they deliver a ransom demand instead of Nita."

"You've got a real dark streak, Linus."

The airship, low to the waves, drew nearer, revealing itself in the dim light of night. There had been good deal more repair work done to the ship since last they'd seen it. One whole side had been replaced with new planking, and it had what looked to be an entirely new envelope. A new and particularly sturdy-looking gig replaced the one that had held their salesman last month. Crew appeared at the railing on either side and threw skillfully tied loops over each of three mooring stones. A few grinding noises came from inside the ship, and down came the gig.

When it was low enough, Linus and Drew were able to see that it held not one person but two. The first was Lil, wearing a mildly ill-fitting dress of elegant Calderan design. The other was Nita, outfitted in her standard work clothes.

"Drew! I'm so glad to find you here! I was afraid I would have to wait until after your shift!" Nita called down as the gig continued to lower down to the water.

"I traded shifts. I wanted to get you away from these people as soon as possible," Drew said. He looked to Lil. "No offense."

"Aw heck. I'm pretty sure the bad influence went both ways, Mister," Lil replied.

Nita leapt from the gig a few feet before it reached the water and landed in the skiff. "How has everything been since I've been gone?"

"Well, the foreman is pretty sore you took your relief time for the whole year at once without notice, but no one seems to think anything much of your sudden trip otherwise. You've always been a little impulsive."

"And my mother?"

"I understand she's been holding on, but your sister says she's in a bad way."

"Listen, I need a favor. I know you came here to do your monthly trading, and I assure you there are better goods today than you've ever seen before, but I need you to take me back to Tellahn immediately."

"You got the medicine?"

"I did. And I've got to get to my mother. The sooner she gets it the better."

#

Nita hurried into her gorgeous home. The glorious joy of homecoming could wait; the task at hand was too important. She rushed to her mother's bedside.

"Mother!" she urged, shaking her gently.

"What? Eh? Who's there?" the sleeping matriarch asked groggily.

"Nita? Is that you?" asked her father, awakened by the noise. "Where have you been? You can't just go running off."

"I know, Father, and I'm sorry. Mother, please, come with me."

"You know your mother needs her rest," Mr. Graus said.

"Mother, what do you know about the people of Rim?"

"Precious little, and I don't care to learn more."

"Well, I think that's a mistake, and I'll show you why."

She went to her mother's master bath and fetched a glass and a pitcher of cool water. She filled the glass, then revealed a small jar and dumped a carefully measured spoonful into it. She stirred until the powder dissolved.

"Drink this. It will make you well again."

"How could it, dear?"

"Please, Mother. Just drink it."

The matriarch looked into the pleading eyes of her daughter, then reached out with a shaking hand. Nita guided the cup to her mother's lips and steadied her hands enough for her to finish the glass. She then struck a match and lit the bedside lamp.

"Show me your hands," Nita said.

Mrs. Graus held out her delicate hands. They were shaking and unsteady.

"You shouldn't get your mother's hopes up like that, Amanita," said Mr. Graus.

"I… I think…" Mrs. Graus began, tears forming in her eyes. The tremor in her fingers was subsiding. By the time a minute had passed, they were still. "How did you do it?" she asked, forcing the words past the lump in her throat.

"It is a treatment, from a group of terrible but brilliant people. This first dose should take away the symptoms. Two more should cure the disease."

"Are we certain it is safe? Her hands have steadied before. How do we know the drug is actually working?"

"It is working, Caldwell. I can feel it. I can feel it in my hands. My fingers. My arms. My whole body. I haven't felt so calm, so still, in *years*."

"I've spent the last few weeks reading through the books I… acquired on the drug, Mother. I even tested a few doses on myself to be sure it wasn't dangerous. You'll be well again." There were tears in her own eyes now. "In two days, after two more doses, you'll be well."

The mother and daughter embraced tightly, tears running down their faces. When they separated again the joy of the moment and of the reunion began to subside, and the questions asserted themselves.

"How did you get this medicine, dear? Did you go to Rim? How did you get there? And when did you last bathe, dear? You smell a bit off. You know hygiene is important to good health."

Nita laughed and brushed her tears away. "It is a long, long story, Mother."

#

Once she'd taught her mother how to finish her own treatment and left more than enough of the medicine to do so, Nita went about making some preparations. She fetched two more changes of work clothes and a few more suitable outfits for those rare moments when she would not be working. Next came a quick jaunt back to the steamworks, where she replaced those tools that had been lost from her tool sash and grabbed a few she'd wished she'd had during her repairs. She traded in a few favors for a mound of replacement piping, gaskets, and valves, and said her good-byes to her friends and coworkers. Finally she fetched a few items she knew her crewmates would appreciate, including a few fine dresses of the proper size for Lil, a bottle of brandy for Coop, and some Calderan cigars for the captain.

When all was in readiness, she wished her family a tearful good-bye. She promised to come home and visit with each monthly stop from the *Wind Breaker* until she was finished teaching them what they needed to know about its upkeep. Her father promised to do his best to open discussions about reopening the borders, at least for the *Wind Breaker* and her crew. Far too soon, the night was ending and it was time to return to the ship. Linus and Drew took her back to Moor Spires, where Coop and Lil were just closing a deal with one of the other Calderans eagerly seeking exotic goods.

"Oh, you're back! And right on time," Lil said. "We had a good night!"

"Glad to hear it. Did the boiler give you any trouble while I was gone?"

"Believe it or not, we *did* get along without you for quite a few years," Gunner called from above. "Now step into the gig. We've only just got the last planks replaced. I don't want those guns of yours ruining all of that hard work."

"Not so fast. Coop, make sure these two get what they came for. They were a tremendous help to me today."

"Will do, Nita."

"Lil, can you give me a hand with this stuff?"

"Did you get all of the stuff the cap'n asked for?"

"And plenty more."

The women got to work filling the gig with all of the goods Nita had been able to secure, while Coop helped Drew and Linus find what they were after. When everything was loaded and all trades had been made, Nita smiled and hopped into the gig.

"So long, Drew, Linus," she called out. "See you in a month! Oh! Any special requests?"

"I, er… well, I'm looking for a bit more inspiration for my photographs. Perhaps if I could see a few more examples?" he stammered.

"I'll take care of you, Drew," Cooper assured him. "We're heading east this time. You ain't *seen* a woman until you've seen the women they got over there."

The gig, with its haul of traded goods, rose up to the ship's belly. Lil and Nita made their way to the deck and went to work unmooring from the spires.

"So, did the medicine work?" Lil asked.

"It did," Nita said.

"Was it worth coming out here into this mess?"

"Absolutely."

"How was your visit?"

"It was nice to see the familiar faces again, but it's also nice to be back on the *Wind Breaker*."

"Don't tell me you missed this rickety old wreck."

"Well, Caldera is beautiful, and it will always be my home… but what can I say? Once you've had a taste of the sky, the land just seems so small."

"Couldn't have said it better myself. Say, I recognized most of that stuff we loaded up from Caldera, but there were some funny lookin' casks and tools. What were those about?"

"Well, Lil, I *am* a Calderan. In my homeland they say we are all born with at least one great masterpiece inside us, and we owe it to the world to let it out before our days are done. If I'm going to be aboard the *Wind Breaker*, let *her* be my masterpiece. Just wait until you see what I've got in mind…"

With that, they hauled in the ropes, set their course, and were once again on their way.

###

From The Author

Thank you for reading this fun little experiment. *Free-Wrench* was a National Novel Writing Month project. It went from concept to completion in less than three months. As my first foray into Steampunk, it was a lot of fun to write, and if you enjoyed it, please consider reading some of my other books. If you enjoyed the story, or if you felt it could use some work, please feel free to contact me through any of the methods listed in the next section. I'm always happy to get feedback, and I do my best to answer any messages I get from my readers. Thanks for reading!

Discover other titles by Joseph R. Lallo:

The Book of Deacon Series:

Book 1: *The Book of Deacon*
Book 2: *The Great Convergence*
Book 3: *The Battle of Verril*
Book 4: *The D'Karon Apprentice*

Other stories in the same setting:

Jade
The Rise of the Red Shadow

The Big Sigma Series:

Book 1: *Bypass Gemini*
Book 2: *Unstable Prototypes*
Book 3: *Artificial Evolution*

NaNoWriMo Projects:

The Other Eight
Free-Wrench
Skykeep

Connect with Joseph R. Lallo

Website: www.bookofdeacon.com
Twitter: @jrlallo
Tumblr: jrlallo.tumblr.com

Made in the USA
Middletown, DE
19 January 2023